Praise for *Emmy in the Key of Code*

★ "As Emmy learns Java, the language and structure of programming seep into her poems. Music and code interweave. . . . And readers will cheer to see them work collectively . . . to create something beautiful."
—*Kirkus Reviews*, starred review

"This timely debut . . . champions girls in STEM and delivers a positive message about being 'always yourself.' . . . Through the author's creative mesh of coding, music, poetry, and narrative, this story uniquely conveys the art and beauty that can be found in multiple disciplines. . . . Relatable and relevant." —*Publishers Weekly*

"This unusual tale seamlessly weaves basic computer coding concepts into a compelling story about middle schoolers struggling to forge their own identities in spite of the expectations of their families and society." —*School Library Journal*

"*Emmy in the Key of Code* is a story about taking risks—about the risk of reaching out to a new friend, the risk of choosing a new place, the risk of forgiveness, and, most especially, the risk of embracing a whole new way of imagining and expressing your life. It's thrilling to watch Emmy take these risks—and just as thrilling to watch Aimee Lucido ask her readers to do the same in this novel as innovative in its language as it is satisfying in its story." —Gary Schmidt, Newbery Honor–winning author of *The Wednesday Wars*

Emmy in the Key of Code

CODE

Emmy in the Key of Code

Aimee Lucido

Versify

Houghton Mifflin Harcourt

Boston   New York

Versify® is an imprint of Houghton Mifflin Harcourt Publishing Company. Versify
is a registered trademark of Houghton Mifflin Harcourt Publishing Company.

hmhbooks.com

The text was set in Helvetica Neue.
Typography by Celeste Knudsen

The Library of Congress has cataloged the hardcover edition as follows:
Names: Lucido, Aimee, author.
Title: Emmy in the key of code / by Aimee Lucido.
Description: Boston ; New York : Houghton Mifflin Harcourt, [2019] |
Summary: Sixth-grader Emmy tries to find her place in a new school and to
figure out how she can create her own kind of music using a computer.
Identifiers: LCCN 2018053060
Subjects: | CYAC: Novels in verse. | Computer programming—Fiction. |
Sexism—Fiction. | Middle schools—Fiction. | Schools—Fiction. | Composition
(Music)—Fiction. | Moving, Household—Fiction. | Family life—California—San
Francisco—Fiction. | San Francisco (Calif.)—Fiction.
Classification: LCC PZ7.5.L82 Emm 2019 | DDC [Fic]—dc23
LC record available at https://lccn.loc.gov/2018053060

ISBN: 978-0-358-04082-8 hardcover
ISBN: 978-0-358-43462-7 paperback

Manufactured in the United States of America
DOC 10 9 8 7 6 5 4 3 2 1
4500821650

To Baker Franke and Laura Ruby:

the original Ms. Delaneys

California Dreaming

I'd never visited California before we moved here
but I'd heard about it
in songs.

Mom even made a playlist
and she and Dad sang along
the whole drive over from Wisconsin
but even after three days straight of
    Katy Perry
    the Beach Boys
    the Mamas & the Papas
I still didn't believe it.
Why would people here be different
than anywhere else?

But now that I'm here
on the first day of sixth grade at my new school
the hallway is full of kids
tapping on cell phones that probably cost more
than an entire month's rent
in our new house.

Plus
everyone looks like they just jumped off the cover
of a magazine.

Hipster glasses
jeans where the only holes
were put there on purpose
and everyone pulling out a reusable container
full of weird grains
that must be their lunch.

I tug down my Packers hoodie
because it's colder here
than the Beach Boys promised
and this way no one can see
that I look nothing like
the cover of
a magazine.

I wish San Francisco
would go back
to just being
a song.

Pretending

As I walk down the hallway
I head-hum my favorite walking song.
Beethoven's Minuet in G.
dum dee dum dee dum dee dum dee dum

I move **andante**
matching my steps to the beat
left, and right, and left, and right, and left

so I can pretend
I'm not at all sore
from climbing up the hill in front of the school.
left, and right, and left, and right, and left

I can pretend I've been hiking it my whole life.
left, and right, and left, and right, and left

I can pretend I don't smell like Wisconsin
and that I wore the right clothes to school today
and that I'm going to make tons of friends
and have an amazing year
left, and right, and left, and right, and left

just like everyone else.

Locker Number 538

Finally I reach my locker
    12 clockwise
    32 counterclockwise
    8 clockwise

                Stuck.

Attempted Duet No. 1

"Hi, I'm new here. My name is—"

"That's my locker."

Sorry About That

I look up at the locker number
engraved in metal at the top.
583.

                              Whoops.

   left, and right, and left, and right, and left

Homeroom

The desks are full of kids talking
laughing and shouting
in harmony.

Quartets
trios
a few duets here and there.
Even the teacher runs around
in a stunning rendition of
"Flight of the Bumblebee."

Everyone must have practiced their parts
all summer long
because they perform them perfectly
no matter if they're the background vocals
or the lead singer.

But there's no part for me.

There's no group for girls wearing Packers hoodies
because they forgot to ask their mom
if they could go back-to-school shopping.

There is no group for girls carrying brown paper bags
stuffed with white bread sandwiches

and full-fat potato chips
because they made their grocery run at Safeway
instead of Whole Foods.

There is no group for girls who should have asked
to live with their grandma and grandpa
back in Wisconsin
so they could stay at the school
where they knew their part
backwards and forward.

Here in homeroom I feel like
                                    a wrong
                  note.

Attempted Duet No. 2

"Hi, I'm new here. My name is—"

                              "You're sitting at my desk."

Solo

Isn't the teacher supposed to invite me
to the front of the classroom?

Isn't she supposed to ask me where I came from
and when I moved here
and what's my
favorite flavor
of ice cream?

Isn't she supposed to give me a desk buddy?
Or a member of student council to show me around?
Or at the very least shouldn't there be somebody
anybody
other than me
who doesn't already
belong?

Shouldn't someone at least ask my name?

Attempted Duet No. 3

"Hi, I'm new here. My name is—"

> "Sorry, dear, give me a minute.
> I need to find
> the elective sign-up sheets."

Hazy

In Wisconsin
the first day of school was always hot
and muggy
far too long and far too bright.

It always used to make me think of Ella Fitzgerald
singing "Summertime."

But here
in San Francisco
in homeroom
I stare out the window
waiting for class to start
and Ella Fitzgerald isn't singing "Summertime."
She's singing "Lost in a Fog."

When our homeroom teacher claps
her hands
starting class
I'm relieved.

I was getting dizzy
staring out into all that fog.

By the Way . . .

. . . my name is Emmy.

None of the Above

In fifteen minutes
I am supposed to decide
where I go
Monday   Wednesday   Friday
before lunch.

A. _____ Symphony Orchestra and Choir
B. _____ Winter Play: *A Tale of Two Cities*
C. _____ Cooking Around the World
D. _____ Introduction to Computer Science

In fifteen minutes
I am supposed to decide
who I am.

A. _____ Musician
B. _____ Actor
C. _____ Chef
D. _____ Geek

But never before
have I felt more like

option E.

Option A

I picture myself three times a week
in option A.

Music class.
That's where I'm supposed to be.

Dad's a pianist.
Mom's an opera singer.
Even my own heartbeat thumps in three-quarter time:
    boom-bah-dah
    boom-bah-dah
    boom.

I can't remember a time before music.
I don't think I ever existed without it.
I was born with it like a twin
or a vital organ.
Music swims in my bloodstream
burrows in between my bones
and if it disappeared
I'm not sure what would be left.

I'd like to call myself a musician
but after nine years of lessons

from piano
      to flute
           to violin
                 to voice
                      to saxophone
                             to drums
                                    to bass
                                         to guitar

when we moved to San Francisco we gave up.
I'm no good.

Turns out loving music
isn't the same as being a musician.

I should sign up for the winter play
or Cooking Around the World
or Introduction to Computer Science
but how can I sign up for something else
when all I want
is to be a
musician?

Empty

I look around the room
at the other kids
trading papers with their friends
making sure they're writing the same options
in the same order.

I don't have anyone to trade papers with
and I don't fit anywhere on the sheet
so I leave my future up to fate.

While the teacher is still handing out papers
I turn mine in
blank.

What I Hear from Across the Room

"Everyone, make sure you sign up for music."

"Okay!"   "Okay!"   "Yeah, okay, I guess so."

"What do you mean, you guess so?"

"Well, it's just
that's a lot of singing."

"Isn't that the point?"

"I mean
we already have SFCC after school
and concerts for that.
It's already kind of a lot."

"Yeah but don't you want to get into
the Honey Bees?"

"Well . . ."

"My sister does say the Honey Bees give priority
to girls who are in the middle school choir."

"Besides, what else would we even take?
Cooking?"

"It could be fun to do something different
like the play or something."

"Or computers?"

"I can't believe we're even having this conversation.
We're signing up for music,
end of discussion."

"Okay!"   "Okay!"   "Yeah, okay, I guess so."

The Girl in Braids

When all my classmates
except me
have scattered
a voice from down the hallway
reaches me:
  "I left my headphones! I'll catch up with you later."

So says a girl
a back-to-class girl
a whispering   chattering   giggling girl.
The *"Yeah, okay, I guess so"* girl.

Now she's back sifting through papers
searching   searching   searching . . .

and I can't help but see
her headphones
peeking from her back pocket
where they never left.

She lifts her paper she
takes a deep breath she
erases.

Replaces her ranking
1, 2, 3, 4
with
4, 3, 2, 1.

She catches me looking
lifts her finger to her mouth and

Shhhh!

The Cafeteria

Dad's piano is a baby grand.
It's yellow
and missing the top key.
He's had it since he first started learning how to play
and he never got a new one.
Not when he signed his first private student
not when he booked his first wedding reception
not even when the piano started to wobble
after Jeopardy
our golden retriever
confused the back leg with dinner.

Mom calls it ugly
but I love it.
It isn't ugly.
It just is.

When something stands out
you look at it funny.
You cock your head
    squint your eyes
        twist your mouth
before you get used to it
and it just looks like
itself.

In my old school I wasn't exactly popular
but I had a place to sit
and friends I'd known since forever.
People dressed like me
and talked like me
and ate the same foods as me

                              but here I stand out.

I may as well be an
ugly
yellow
piano.

Spotlight

I've never been able to eat
when I'm nervous.

I must be nervous now
because my first bite of BLT
turns to sand in my mouth.
Dry and flaky
tasting like empty.

I spit it into my napkin.

You'd be nervous too
if you were the only one
in a room full of duets
trios
symphonies

singing a solo.

Standing Out

I dissect my sandwich
rolling bits of bread into marbles
but I drop one in my lap
oozing a mustard smear onto my jeans.

The napkins
are on the other side of the cafeteria
and when I stand up to get one
I knock the table
and all my bread marbles
fall
on the ground
s   c   a   t   t   e   r   i   n   g
tracing a dozen arrows
pointing to the weirdo
who made them.

I sit back down
napkinless
and glue my eyes to what's left of my sandwich.

Are people staring?
       They're probably staring.
              I need to know if they're staring.
So I look up.

Looking Up

When I look up
No one even notices I'm

here.

And that
is even worse.

Attempted Duet No. 4

"Hi, I'm new here. My name is—"

                              "You're sitting at our table."

If You Close Your Eyes

The Beatles
The Monkees
The Turtles
The Cars
Madonna
Rihanna
Adele
Bruno Mars

Schubert and Schumann
and Chopin
and Bach
Spamalot
Hamilton
Rent
Schoolhouse Rock.

The Vienna Boys Choir
The Philharmonic
Yo-Yo Ma
Miley Cyrus
Taylor Swift
(and my favorite)
Lady Gaga!

So maybe I have no friends
and eat under the stairs
but wearing my headphones
I kind of don't care.
When I have music
nothing matters at all
and anywhere
everywhere
can be
Carnegie Hall.

Elective Assignments

At the end of the day
we go back to homeroom
where we are handed slips of paper
no bigger than a gum wrapper.

Elective assignments.

Around me fly cries of
   "Yes!"   "No!"   "You?"   "Same!"

I look at my slip and see

```
Computer Science: Frankie Delaney HT210
```

And I guess that settles it.
For the first time in my life
I'm not taking piano lessons with Dad
or voice lessons with Mom
or guitar lessons with the music teacher at my old school
and now
I'm not even in the Symphony Orchestra and Choir.

It's official.
I'm not a musician.

Cacophony

Through the chorus of kids comparing classes
shouting:
   "Yes!"   "No!"   "You?"   "Same!"

A melody floats above the choir:
   "Computer science—?"

It's the girl from before
the one with all the braids
and she's trying to make her voice droop
as best she can.

But she's not a very good actor
because even though she's making her voice sound sad
she cannot stop
her smile
from cutting through the classroom concerto
like the trill of a piccolo.

Try Tone

I try to catch her attention
using my friendliest voice
but she is so focused
on harmonizing
with the rest of her string quartet
that she doesn't even notice
me.

The **diminished fifth.**

Attempted Duet No. 5

"Hi, I think we're both in computer science. My name is—"

                              "Maybe they made a mistake?"

"What do you *mean,* you didn't get into music?"

            "Wasn't computer science your last choice?"

   "If it's a mistake
   I'm sure they'll let you change."

                              "Or maybe do the choir without me?"

"Sure, but you can't expect to get into the Honey Bees
if you aren't even in our awful middle school choir."

                                          "Umm . . ."

   "This sucks!
   Now they'll never let Abigail into the Honey Bees!"

"Ugh!
What's the point of even trying out
if Abigail's not on alto."

                        "Hey! I'm an alto!"

"You're no Abigail!"

   "None of us are."

                  "Are you sure
                  you put down music first?"

                                          "Well . . ."

Maybe

The girl in braids
keeps her voice soft
wavering
not quite telling the truth
and not quite lying either.

Her friends tells her
to escalate all the way to the top:
    Principal Fitzgerald.
They're *sure*
that if she explains the situation
the principal will *have* to let her switch.

The girl in braids says:
    "Okay. Maybe I will."

and her friends seem convinced.

But when she stares down
at her elective slip
and smiles
I know that her maybe
is more like
a maybe not.

Fitting In

Mom is beautiful.

She's opera-singer big
strong in the diaphragm
strong in the lungs.
She's a **mezzo**
a Carmen
a Dido
a Princess de Bouillon
and when she sings
her voice
is a roar of applause.

Mom is beautiful
on and off stage.
Even when she's picking me up from school today
next to the magazine moms
in their blue Priuses
even when she sits in our gas guzzler
leaning on the horn
and even when she steps out
wearing her own Packers hoodie
to haul open the trunk
so her not-so-beautiful daughter
can throw in her backpack.

People say we're two peas in a pod
but I don't think so.

Those people just haven't been looking close enough
and they definitely haven't heard me sing.
I sound like
what Jeopardy sounded like
that time he got his tail caught in the car door.

I wish people were right.
That we really were two peas in a pod
because wherever Mom goes
she fits.

Four-four time

Mom is driving me home this week
but starting Monday
I take the train
because Mom has a first day
of her very own.

But for this week
this first week
this first day
I'm glad she's here.

After a day like today
it feels good to be with someone
who marches to the beat
of *my* drum.

So I Don't Worry Her

Before I can click my seat belt
Mom asks:
    "How was it?"

I almost tell her everything.

I almost tell her
how the teacher was so busy
she forgot to introduce me to the class
    how I ate lunch under the stairs
        how I wish California really were
        just a song.
But then I remember
what Mom has told me
nine times since July.

It's a song and dance
so old and familiar
I would sing along
if it were actually a song
(and if I could carry a tune).

So instead of the truth
I say:
    "Fine."

Evening Music

My favorite part
of every day
is four p.m.

When I get home
and I can sit
and tap my toes
and clap along
to any song
Dad wants to play.

Fast and slow and fast again
I watch him bend his bony back
and bop his chin and close his eyes.
The sweat falls down
staccato drops
and I feel better
when he plays.

Griiiiiiiiind

The music changes
and now Dad's playing something new.

Something he's learning for his gig here
as the backup pianist
for the San Francisco Symphony Orchestra.

I don't like it.

It feels clunky and dissonant
and makes me want to grind my teeth.

Even Jeopardy leaves the room.

But it's his dream to play on stage
in front of a sold-out crowd
and that's what we're here for.

This song could be his big break.

So I cover my ears with a pillow
and wait for the song
and wait for the night
and wait for the year
to be over.

Whole Rest

This is the part of the day
when I used to practice piano.

After dinner
when Dad would clean the kitchen
and Mom would be at a show
I'd sit at the keys and try to make them sing.

Mozart's Rondo in C Major
Burgmuller's "By the Limpid Stream"
Beethoven's Sonata, op. 49, no. 2

I'd play and play and play
but no matter how hard I tried
my fingers never matched up
with the music on the page
the music in my head
the music in my heart
the music in my blood.

And don't even get me started
on what would happen
when I'd try to perform.

Now it's eight o'clock
and the house is quiet.

The kitchen is clean
Mom has no rehearsal
and I have nothing to practice

so I lie on the couch
with Jeopardy at my feet
and stare out the window
into the fog.

Option D

Wednesday is the first day of electives
so for fourth period
I look at my slip

    Computer Science: Frankie Delaney, HT210
and navigate my way
to the computer science room.

If I were a musician
I would be in the music tower right now
maybe tuning a school violin
or zinga-zinga-zoo-ing in the choir.
I could be warming up my
lips   teeth   tip of the tongue
on a clarinet.
I could be trying to play something completely new
like the xylophone
or the harmonica
or the harp.
I could be banging on a tambourine
and strumming a bass
and tinging a triangle
but I'm not in the music tower
and I'm not a musician.

I'm in front of HT210.

The Computer Lab

From outside
the room looks shiny and expensive.

Not like the computer lab at my old school
which might as well have been built
with tin cans
shoelaces
and Scotch tape.

No
this one is named after some famous graduate
who probably should never find out
that our class only needs six
of the lab's twenty-five computers
each probably powerful enough
to take us to the moon and back.

Even the classrooms here
feel like they just hopped off the cover
of a magazine.

Back and Forth

I stand outside
pacing.
  left, and right, and left, and right, and left

What if I'm just as awful as a computer scientist
as I am as a musician?
What if the girl in braids is mad
that I caught her changing her elective?
What if computers are boring
and the teacher is mean
and I spend my class staring out the window
getting lost in the fog?
  left, and right, and left, and right, and left

I took extra time this morning getting dressed.
I wore the only jeans I have
that look almost new.
They have only one hole in them
and it's just on the ankle
so you can barely see it.

Way better than yesterday.

But what if my jeans weren't the problem
and even after all this effort

I still stand out
like an ugly yellow piano?
left, and right, and left, and right, and left

The clock ticks
                    11:14
and if I wait any longer
I'm late.
left, and right, and left, and right, and left

I inhale like Mom does
when she's about to sing a high G
and walk inside.

Standing Out: Remix

I collapse in a swivel chair
in front of an I SPEAK JAVA poster
and there
sitting next to me
is the girl in braids.

I feel weird making eye contact.
She knows I know about the elective slips
and what if she hates me for that?
What if she saw me pacing outside
and can tell how out of place I feel?

But worst of all
what if she barely even notices I'm here?

So I delay the inevitable
by spending forever adjusting my backpack on the ground
which I should never have done
because of course a strap catches on my chair
which I have to kneel down on the floor to fix
which gets stuck further when I try to pull it out
which I only manage to unstick by

rolling the chair
back and forth
        back and forth
                back and forth
and by the time I sit back in my seat
my knees are covered in floor
my hands smell like swivel chair
and to top it all off
my jeans have slipped down
and the top of my underwear is showing.

Is the girl in braids staring?
        She's probably staring.
            I need to know if she's staring.

So I look up.

Blending In

Instead of staring
the girl in braids
wears a smile so sure
that I know
she doesn't think I stand out
like an ugly yellow piano
at all.

In fact
it seems that
the only thing she thinks I look like
is myself.

< 48 >

Duet No. 1

"I'm Abigail. What's your name?"

> "Hi, I'm new here.
> My name is Emmy."

Something True

The teacher **crescendoes** in
with a smile painted candy-apple red.
A color so joyful
so **allegro**
so **dolce** and **vivace**
that it spills onto the rest of her face
and when she sings:

    "Welcome to Introduction to Computer Science!
    You can call me Ms. Delaney
    and I am SO excited you're here!"

I actually believe her.

Polyrhythm

There's this part in Mozart's *Don Giovanni*
when one orchestra is playing in three-four time
while a second orchestra plays in two-four time.

I always thought it sounded confused.
Like two people
trying to have a conversation
while reading different pages
of sheet music.

I hadn't thought about it in a while
but that's the song that plays in my head
when a kid walks into class
sees Ms. Delaney at the whiteboard
writing her name

    Frankie Delaney

and asks:
    "Where's Mr. Delaney?"

Orchestra One vs. Orchestra Two

"Where's Mr. Delaney?"

                              "There isn't one."

"But my elective slip says
 Frankie Delaney HT210."

                              "Yep! Welcome to class!"

"No, no, you don't understand.
 I'm looking for
 the computer science teacher."

                              "You're looking at her!"

"But—"

                              "But what?"

"Are you serious?"

                              "So serious."

"Well, that's weird."

                              "I don't see why it would be."

"I mean, you're—"

                              "You're Francis, right?"

"Yeah, how did you—"

                              "Please sit down.
                              Class started two minutes ago
                              and it seems like we have so much to learn
                              that we can't waste another moment."

Fun Facts

First there's Iain Makropoulos
who is taller than the teacher.
Fun fact:
> Last year he was the fifth grade record holder
> for the hundred-meter dash.

Second is Drake Adler
with an earring made out of a dangling shark's tooth.
Fun fact:
> He once wrote a service in C++.

> Whatever that means.

Then goes Evan Wu
with hair that is long, long.
Fun fact:
> His mom is making him take this class.

The fourth is Abigail Grant.
The girl in braids.
The giggling girl.
The fun-fact-so-fun-it-pours-out-of-her girl:
> She is a Tetris champion
> and she's been singing
> with the San Francisco Children's Choir

(SFCC for short)
since she was three years old
and she just started programming a little last summer
and loved it so much
that she thinks now she wants to be
the head of a Fortune 500 tech company
by the time she is 25.
And
in the short term
if she doesn't spend her allowance on movie tickets
or on pizza at lunch
then one day
she will save enough money
to buy the parts
to build her own computer.

Not-So-Fun Fact

Ms. Delaney says:
   "Francis.
    It's your turn."

Ever since he sat down
Francis has had his arms tucked tight
under his armpits
like he's afraid to touch anything.
And he wrinkles his nose
as he looks around the room
like he smells salmon
left in the garbage too long.
When he talks
he grumbles
like he's not willing to leave his own orchestra
no matter how out of sync it is
with everyone else
and when it's his turn for his fun fact
I swear
he stares right at me
when he says:
   "My fun fact is that I can't believe that
   this
    is the elective I'm stuck in
    all semester long."

My Turn

The sixth is me
Emmy
whose head is reeling with fun facts.

I could tell everyone that I moved here in August
for my dad's big break
as the new second-in-line pianist for the symphony.

Or I could tell them that my mom
who once sang Mozart in Carnegie Hall
is going to work in an office on Monday
for the first time in twenty-two years.

Or I could tell them about my dog
Jeopardy
who's kind of my twin brother
because he was born just hours
after I was.

I can't wait to talk about any of this
all of this
but when I take a diaphragm breath
to prepare myself
for my solo
my chair scoots a half-inch

to the right
    toward Francis
                who squirms
                away from me
                    like I've got a sickness
                        he doesn't want to catch.

                He makes the face
                the ugly piano face
                and this time
                I know for sure
                it's not in my head.

                He hates me.

Empty: Remix

In the space
that just seconds ago held
fun facts
that I wanted to shout so loud
they could hear me
all the way in
Wisconsin
there is now
nothing
except
blank.

My head fuzzes
my vision spots
my fingers tingle.

I recognize this feeling
I know this feeling
I hate this feeling
so before it gets any worse
I say:
   "I don't have a fun fact."

And Ms. Delaney says:
   "That's okay. You can tell us when you're ready."

< 58 >

Ms. Delaney

Number seven is Ms. Delaney
at the front
with short corkscrew hair
and a dress that skims the carpet
and that **allegro**-colored smile.
So bright
and so bold
she's like the flourish of an electric violin
in the middle of a Beethoven symphony
and she has not one
but three
fun facts:

#1:
This time two years ago she was working
at one of those big tech companies
in the South Bay.
One of those with high salaries
and
like Dad says
even higher
stress.

But
(#2)
she quit
because
"Sometimes life has mixed-up ways
    of telling you where you're NOT supposed to be."

And while her last fun fact might as well be that she's
THRILLED
to be starting teaching this semester
she would be remiss if she didn't mention that
(#3)
she once was on *Who Wants to Be a Millionaire?*
and won $250,000.

Repeat

People seem impressed
that Ms. Delaney was on TV:
   "Were you scared?"

   "Does that mean you're rich?"

   "Does that mean you're famous?"

   "How did you spend all that money?"

But I hardly notice the answers
because I'm still stuck
on the part
where Ms. Delaney is just as new here
as I am.

Muscle Memory

Ms. Delaney says to turn
to our computers
so we can get as much as we can
out of the time that we have left.

Even Francis uncrosses his arms
just long enough
to turn to the computer
and jiggle his mouse
like the rest of us.

The computers wake up
and on each screen
is a window.

Ms. Delaney says that this window
is an Integrated Development Environment
or IDE
and it's where we will do our coding.

But to me all it looks like is
blank.

tap, tap, tap

I type my name in the top left corner
like I do on my English essays
but Ms. Delaney says:
    "Don't type just yet
    because this isn't a word processor
    and writing code is not the same
    as writing an essay.
    But give it time
    and it will flow out of you
    like you were born with it."

Ms. Delaney Says

Memorize this
the code surrounding our first program
as sounds.
As keystrokes.
As a piece of music.
Swimming in our bloodstream
burrowing in between our bones
until we can sing it in our sleep.

public
static
void
main
string
bracket
bracket
args

One day we will learn what it does.
Every word. Every line.
Every note played on the keyboard.

But right now it's okay if it doesn't make sense.
If it's just music
written in the language called Java.

{ }

We type it out
turning the sounds
into code.

```
public static void main(String[] args) {


}
```

Ms. Delaney says this is the entry point
for every single program
in Java.

It makes me think of a time signature
for a piece of music—
how you know where it all starts.

The curly braces here
the {

```
}
```
hold the entire program.
We don't have to understand them fully
quite yet

but I like them because {
    they keep things separate {
        like a colon {
            or measure bars {
                ways of distinguishing one idea {
                    from another {
                        and when they close {}
                  }
                it feels complete
                }
            contained
            }
        finished
        }
    like a double bar
    }
at the end of a song.
}

Hello, World!

For our first program
we write a single instruction:

```
public static void main(String[] args) {
    System.out.println("Hello, World!");
}
```

Ms. Delaney says that's it.
That we wrote a whole program
and all we need to do
is play it.

But I don't see how that's possible.
How could I have written so little
and understood even less
and yet
somehow
have written a program?

I find the little green play button
at the top of the screen
and even though I'm sure
I did something wrong
I press it anyway.

First Words

```
>Hello, World!
```

Lunchtime Music

It's stuck in my head
like a song.

public
static
void
main
string
bracket
bracket
args

I give it a melody
and a back beat
which remixes itself
over my fingers tapping
on my thighs.

PUB-lic
STAT-ic
void, main, string.
BRACK-et
BRACK-et
ARGS!

And while I eat
the pesto and pine nut quinoa
that Mom bought for me
in a last-minute run
to Whole Foods
to replace my Wisconsin food
I sing
under my breath
my whispers echoing beneath the stairs

in my own private
concert hall.

So I Don't Get My Hopes Up

Today when Mom asks {
    "How was your day?"
}

I almost tell her everything.

How the teacher wore lipstick
the color of **allegro**.

How I met Abigail
who's been coding since last summer
and singing since forever.

How maybe California
isn't such a terrible song after all.

But then I remember
Francis
and how he made me feel like I'm an ugly yellow piano

so
once again
I say {
    "Fine."
}

4:00 p.m.

Usually Dad plays piano
the way some dads play golf.

For himself.

But tonight he's not playing
he's *practicing*.

It's that song again
the one that sounds like badly tuned violins
dropped drum kits and rusty tambourines
and your parents telling you
that you're moving away from the only place
you've ever called home.

I still don't like it
but there's something to it.

A rhythm
a bounce
a drumbeat.

With my voice and ears muffled beneath my pillow
and Jeopardy hiding in the kitchen
I sing.

4'33"

There's music in me
I can feel it

surging

      m   g
   u   p   n
j   i

cha-
    cha-
        chaing
So while Dad cooks dinner
and Mom is walking Jeopardy
I
cha-
    cha-
        cha
my way over to the piano.

I sit on the bench
put my hands on the keys

and the music in me

                  disappears

Scenic Route

On Thursdays there is no

PUB-lic
STAT-ic
void, main, string.
BRACK-et
BRACK-et
ARGS!

There is only

homeroom
math
science
lunch
gym
humanities
humanities
spanish

But after science
I take the scenic route
past the computer lab
before eating my lunch
beneath the stairs.

I put on my headphones
to distract
my anxious stomach.
But today
I surprise myself.
I barely even pay attention
to the Vivaldi in my ears
because in spite of Francis
I can't wait to see
what we're going to make in class
tomorrow.

Just Almost

Ms. Delaney gives me another chance
to say my fun fact.

Ms. Delaney grins **allegro**-red
while Abigail sticks up her thumb
and I think maybe I can talk about how last night
I beat my parents for the first time ever at Monopoly.
Or about how Dad thinks this gig
as the backup pianist
is finally going to be his big break.
Or maybe I can say that my favorite ice cream flavor is
lemon cardamom
from Purple Door back home.

I almost talk.
I was ready to talk.
I would have talked
if it wasn't for
a SNORT.

An eye roll of a sound
from an eye roll of a boy

and I don't even need to look up
to see the way he's looking at me.

Stage Fright

Maybe it's pathetic
that all it takes is one little SNORT
to make my larynx freeze up
like I'm about to sing a high note
and I forgot to inhale.

But it's more than just a SNORT
it's how he's looking at me.
A head-cocking
    eye-squinting
        mouth-twisting
look.

It's a look I've seen before
every time I walked on stage
with a cello
or a flute
or a stack of music fit for my voice part.

It's the *You don't belong here* face.

The one that once came
with whispered words {
    "*She's* their daughter?"
    "I would have expected more."

"She doesn't look like she belongs up there
   at all."
}

And now
just like what happened
the last time
I stepped on a stage
before I can perform anything I rehearsed
my mind starts to
f   u   z   z

                              and so I stop
                              before it gets any worse.

Turning Away

After class a voice calls {
    "Abigail!
     We're here to rescue you!"
}

There is a group
a giggling group
a group saying
Choose whose side you want to be on
with folders full of sheet music
dangling down at their sides.

It's the Option A group.
The choir girls group.
The musical group.

The group
that in a world
where I could sing on pitch
might have been my friends.

They say {
    "I'm so mad they didn't let you switch."

"Ms. Sinclair keeps saying
  how much we need more altos."

"I dunno . . .
  something seems weird to me."

"Hey
  it could be worse
  at least *you're* not the one stuck in computer class."
}

I say goodbye
but Abigail must not hear me
because the back-to-class girl
has her back to me.

< 80 >

Don't Belong

I guess Abigail
doesn't want to be my friend.

I guess no one does.

Usually

Usually
used to be a song I knew well.

Usually
I could eat at home.

Usually
all it took was one round of *Moonlight* Sonata
and I could forget about whatever happened
during the school day.

Usually
I could enjoy the lasagna
the garlic bread
the Caesar salad
without my stomach
pretzeling.

Usually.

I must have forgotten the tune to
Usually
when I left Wisconsin.

A Good Weekend

Over the weekend
I let myself forget about school.

Saturday morning
Dad wakes me with Debussy.
I solve a jigsaw puzzle
—the one with the close-up of the hummingbird—
while tapping out the rhythm to Dad's rendition of
Suite bergamasque.

We walk Jeopardy
through Golden Gate Park
with a packed picnic.
It's foggy
as always
but Jeopardy licks at the grass
and I wonder what fog tastes like
so I stick out my tongue
to sip it.

On Sunday
Dad plays Chopin.
Jeopardy splats his front paws
on my shoulders
and we waltz through the kitchen

boom-bah-dah
boom-bah-dah
boom
while Mom records on her phone.

It's a good weekend.

So good
that I almost forget
what comes after Sunday.

Anticipation

Dad makes chili on Sunday night
to celebrate Mom's first day
of work tomorrow.

Chili
with jalapeño cornbread
is our fall treat
even though the weather here
feels more like
the rainy season
than fall.

It's usually my favorite
but today
I can barely eat.
I'm too nervous
worrying about tomorrow
and if I'll ever
find anyone
who wants to be my friend.

But Dad takes his third bowl
and asks
did he make it too spicy?

There's never leftovers
on chili night.

Mom sighs
stirs up the kidney beans
the ground beef
the sour cream.
She takes a bite
then stirs some more.

Maybe I'm not the only one
nervous about tomorrow.

Songs in the Key of Life

When I was little
three
maybe four years old
we had a record player in our basement.

The records were always dusty
crackly
but when I'd get sad
Mom and Dad would play me this song
called "Sir Duke"
about how music is the one language
that everyone speaks
and you can tell because
as soon as it starts to play
everyone can feel it.

We'd listen to this song over and over and over again
singing
dancing
clapping our hands
until I couldn't even remember
what it was that had made me sad.

So this morning
as I walk up a hill

to take a bus
to the train
to another hill
to school
I listen to the song.

I let the words rush through me
feeling it all over
and in the quiet of my head
I am singing
I am singing
I am singing.

Give Me Time

Today Ms. Delaney asks
once again
if I'm ready to share my fun fact.

But I don't need to look at Francis
to know that he's still crossing his arms
like he doesn't want to risk touching me
to know that he's still crinkling his nose
like I smell like rotting salmon.

And I don't need Francis's face
to know
that if I try
to say my fun fact
my head is going to fuzz
so I say {
    "How about I tell you
      when I'm ready."
}

Ms. Delaney's smile
paints a cherry streak in the air
and she says {
    "Sounds good to me!"
}

Building Blocks

Ms. Delaney says this week we will be learning
primitive types.

Primitive types are the programming bits that exist
without us having to play a single note
on our keyboard.

They are the pieces that come built-in.

The building blocks
for every single program
in the whole world.

She says with these primitive types
we have the power
to make anything we could ever want.
Games.
    Robots.
        Music.

Francis
without even looking at anyone
says {
    "Not a spaceship."
}

But Ms. Delaney doesn't even pause—she just
shrugs and says {
   "Why not?"
}

And so we spend the period
stacking building blocks
trying to reach the moon.

Purple

Ms. Delaney gives us eight words
and tells us to type them on our screens.

I type
like I used to play **scales**.
Carefully.
Training my fingers.

In my head
the words feel like nonsense.

```
int
    char
        short
            long
                boolean
                    byte
                        double
                            float
```

See?
Nonsense.

But when I type them
they turn purple on my screen

and the nonsense
becomes music
taking shape right before my eyes.

It's like the computer just smiled at me
and said {
    "Hello, Emmy!
    I see what you're doing.
    I see.
    I see you."
}

Booleans

My favorite building block
is a boolean.
I roll the word around in my mouth
like it's a caramel candy.
boo-lee-in.

A boolean is like
a Lego
with only one bump.
It's the smallest building block
and it represents
either true
or false.

I look around the room
at Ms. Delaney's you-belong-here smile
at Abigail's you-belong-here thumbs-up

at Francis's
you-don't-belong-here
SNORT

and I wish everything
could be boolean.

Hopes

Mom gets home from her first day of work
around six.
I ask {
   "How was it?"
}

and she says {
   "Fine."
}

I hope her "fine"
is better than mine.

I hope Mom's boss took her around the office
and introduced her
to his other assistants.

I hope she didn't try to sit
at the wrong desk.

I hope they had freezers full
of her favorite flavor of ice cream
and that when they asked for her fun fact
she said {
   "I'm an opera singer

and my family just moved here in August
because my husband just got his big break
as the new second-in-line pianist
for the San Francisco Symphony Orchestra."
}

And most of all
I hope Mom finds someone
to calm her nervous stomach
when she finds that her new job
is not quite
boolean.

Boolean Logic

Things that are true {
    Yes, I would like to watch
        Toddlers in Tiaras with you tonight.
    Yes, I have walked Jeopardy.
    Yes, I would love to try that new ramen place
        in Berkeley this weekend.
    Yes, I will take out the garbage after dinner.
}

        Things that are false {
            No, I don't have too much homework.
            No, I have plans Saturday morning
                and can't help you unpack the
                garage.
            No, I didn't scuff the kitchen wall.
                Must have been Jeopardy.
            No, it wasn't me who finished the milk
                and didn't throw away the carton.
                Must have been . . .
                Jeopardy?
                }
        Things that are not quite boolean {
            Ummm . . .
        school today was
            fine?
            }

What If?

We spend the rest of the week
playing with `boolean`s
stacking our Lego pieces
into bigger and bigger buildings.
Note   by note   by note
our fingers build
scales   **chords**   **arpeggios.**

Programs.

We learn about `if`
which Ms. Delaney says is
a useful little question
because it can only be
`true`   or   `false`.

I don't raise my hand and ask
What about the in-betweens?
What about the things that are not so `boolean`?
What about the things that don't feel
`true`   but also don't feel   `false`?

I don't ask about them
because in Java
those things don't matter.

If/Then

if (I walk into the cafeteria
    and I sit at an empty table
    and I open up my lunchbox
    and pull out my lentil salad) {
        I will see Francis at his table
        with his head cocks
        his eye squints
        his mouth twists.
        I will see Francis's face
        and not be able to eat
        at all.
} else if (I stay under the stairs
    and I listen to Billie Holiday's "Blue Moon"
    and Tchaikovsky's Piano Concerto No. 1
    and Jimi Hendrix's "Purple Haze") {
        I can sit by myself
        and eat my lunch
        and look forward
        to spending the weekend
        learning
        about computers.
}

My Hand-Me-Down Laptop

What's inside of it?
Strings? Bits? Magic?—I wish I
could find Mom's pliers.

Why I Didn't Destroy My Laptop

Screwdriver
pliers
a pair of wire cutters
and a thirty-nine-minute
video.

Turns out I need a computer
to figure out
how to take one apart.

Java

is a language
I am learning to speak
and to understand
like Spanish   or French   or Mandarin.

But Java isn't
like Spanish   or French   or Mandarin
at all.

Java is like Pig Latin
because it's an ecret-say anguage-lay
that not many people speak.

There are hundreds of computer languages
but Java is mine.

Just saying it feels like a chocolatey drop
on my tongue
and I spend the weekend
on my laptop
wrapped in a blanket
fingers twitching
at all the things
I want to use this language
to say.

Languages

Racket, Ruby, Groovy, Scheme,
Scala, Rust, Objective C,
Python, Pascal, Prolog, Perl,
Pico, Logo, Haskell, Curl,
PHP, CSS, XML, D
HTML, X++, SQL, C
Go, Hack, Lingo, Lava

Java   Java   Java   Java

For What It's Worth . . .

. . . we did eat dinner
at that new ramen place in Berkeley
and it was incredible.

The Things I Almost Say

Today I am ready to say my fun fact.

I want to talk about my weekend
and how I spent so much time
researching the weirdest programming languages.
I want to tell the class {
    Did you know
    that there is a language called Shakespeare
    and when you read it out loud
    it sounds like a long-ago play?
    And that there is a language called Whitespace
    that is nothing but blank?
    Oh and also I have a dog named Jeopardy
    and I posted a video of us waltzing on YouTube
    and it already has over a thousand views.
}
I want to say—
But then {
    SNORT
}
Ms. Delaney says {
    "Bless you."
} and hands Francis a Kleenex.
But it wasn't a sneeze
and so I don't say anything.

Making a Mark

I don't say anything for the rest of class.
Even when Ms. Delaney calls on me
I just shrug
and wonder
how am I the only one
who notices?

How does no one notice
that Francis
rolls his eyes whenever I move
SNORTs
whenever I speak
and
s   u   r   s
    q   i   m
every
time
I come close.

How am I
the only one
who notices?

Not Just Me

Before I leave the classroom
Abigail catches me by the arm {
   "I don't understand it either.
    Francis, I mean.
    Why he's such a jerk all the time."
}

My throat catches
too tight to talk.

And it would have been enough
her noticing
but Abigail keeps talking {
   "At least you know it's not just you he's mean to."
}

I must not look convinced
because Abigail says {
   "Watch Francis
    the next time
    Ms. Delaney
    makes a mistake
    on the whiteboard."
}

From down the hall
comes a chorus of {
    "Abigail!
      We're here to rescue you!"
} and Abigail
turns her back to me.

But before she walks down the hall
with the Option A Girls
she whispers
so no one else can hear {
    "Trust me."
}

Eye Roll

Now that I see it
I can't un-see it.
Francis rolls his eyes at everything.

Well not everything.

Me   Abigail   Ms. Delaney.

The three of us
girls.

Every time we make a mistake
every time we laugh too loud
every time we move
just a little too close to him
he cocks his head
and squints his eyes
and twists his mouth and
s   u   r   s
    q   i   m

                    to get as far away from us
                    as possible.

Maybe it's not just me
that Francis hates.

4:00 p.m.

Tonight when Dad is playing
it's still the brand-new song.
But this time though I grind my teeth
the **chords** don't sound as wrong.
And yes I'd rather Mozart
but WOW the beat is strong
I find my toes are tapping
and I whisper-sing along.

Two-Part Harmony

Mom calls at six thirty
to say she won't make it home in time
for dinner.

Dad smiles
says {
    "Welcome back to the grind!"
}

Looks like dinner tonight
is just going to be
a duet.

Soup or Salad

Today is Tuesday
which means during lunch
the computer lab should be full of the gamer boys.
However.
Today on the scenic route
I hear no boys.
Instead I hear
girls {

    "So *and* means both have to be true

     and *or* means at least one?"

}
{

    "That's right! So the next time you're at a restaurant

     and the waiter asks if you want soup *or* salad . . ."

}
{

    "I can just say yes!"

}

I hear laughing
Abigail laughing
and Ms. Delaney laughing
and maybe I smile a bit too.

Though I'm not sure that I get the joke.

Don't Tell

I think about the joke
from lunch yesterday
soup *or* salad
as I sit in class on Wednesday.

I don't get it
but I'd like to.

So I ask Abigail.

But Abigail doesn't find it so funny anymore.

Her voice is like a violin string
snapping {
    "Where did you hear that?

    Please don't tell anyone I was there."
}

Back

They're back again.
The giggling group.
The choir girls group.
The *"We're here to rescue you"* group.

The {
    "You don't have to go to music theory
     at lunch again
     like yesterday?"
} group.

I can't say
it doesn't hurt
to see them here.

The could-have-been group.
The should-have-been group.
The would-have-been-you-if-you-just-could-sing group.

But it doesn't hurt
nearly so much
as the back-to-class girl
(the one who smiled so big
when she became her own
Option A)

saying something
that sounds an awful lot
like a lie. {
    "No.
     Music theory is just
     Tuesdays and Thursdays at lunch.
     Yesterday and tomorrow.
     Thank you for rescuing me!"
}

Emails: Opus 1

My inbox is full
of emails from teachers
alerting us
that even though our midterm projects
aren't due until
midterm
that doesn't mean we shouldn't start working on them
yesterday.

My inbox is full
of pictures
of shouting students
at our latest basketball game
wearing yellow and brown
—Go Bumblebees!—
in the daily *Hive Mind*.

My inbox
has one unread email
(1)
from Abigail.

Subject: Soup or Salad

Dear Emmy,

Soup or salad is funny because, in Java, "or" means "at least one." So if a waiter says "Do you want soup or salad?" and you want either soup or salad, then you can just say "yes" because you do want soup or salad! What the waiter means is "Would you rather have soup or salad?" but that's never what they say!

—Ab Fab

P.S. "or" in Java is written like this: || and "and" is written like this: &&. Ms. Delaney will teach us this next week but now you're ahead of everyone else!

P.P.S. You should come to the computer lab tomorrow during lunch. Ms. Delaney is teaching us websites!

P.P.P.S. Please don't tell Rebecca and Divya and Angel that I'm there. Not that you would. It's just that I kind of lied about signing up for computer science class in the first place. They think it's a mistake that I ended up there and if they knew I was taking extra classes they may figure it all out. So I tell them I'm at music theory and they'd never forgive me so just . . . please don't tell.

Both

That night
when Dad asks {
   "Do you want spinach
    or string beans?"
} I smile and say {
   "Yes!"
}

If/Then: Remix

```
if ( It's before lunchtime on Thursday ) {
    look forward to lunchtime on Thursday.
}
```

Come On In

I keep my hope
asleep
on Thursday
and tell myself that I'm taking the scenic route
on the way to the staircase
from science class.

I walk through the halls
holding Abigail's email on the edge of my mind
searching for voices.
dum dee dum dee dum dee dum dee dum

And sure enough
when I pass the door to the room {
    "See? If you change the CSS
    you can refresh the page and . . ."
}

{
    "Whoa!"
}

I walk inside like I'm a **chord**
resolving.

The Computer Lab: Remix

Today there are no boys
no sneers
no whispers
no SNORTs.

The only sound
is our voices
accompanied by the tips of our fingers
tapping in three-quarter time
as Ms. Delaney shows us
    me and Abigail
    Abigail and me
what to type
to get the screen to paint
pictures out of pixels.

Innate

I can't remember a time before music.

I can't remember the first time I heard
  "Mary Had a Little Lamb"
  "Clair de Lune"
  "Rhapsody in Blue."

I can't remember the first time Dad played
Beethoven's Minuet in G
the first time Mom sang
Carmen's habanera.
The first time we played "Sir Duke"
on the old record player.

Before this year
all my friends were like songs that I knew by heart.

I can't remember meeting them.
I can't remember choosing to be friends.
I can't remember the time before.

But with Abigail and Ms. Delaney
talking and laughing and typing
I wonder if maybe the best songs
are the ones you learn to love.

Dad's Song: 4:00 p.m.

is a rumbling song
a grumbling song
a twisting and turning and tumbling song.
It's a toe-tapping song
a butt-shaking song
a dog-dancing
rip-rolling
fun
fun
fun
song.

How could I ever have hated this song?

The New Schedule

```
if ( It's lunchtime )  {
    if ( It's Monday || Wednesday || Friday )  {
        go straight to the staircase after class
        && listen to Queen's "Don't Stop Me Now"
        && listen to Bach's Well-Tempered Clavier
        && listen to Tupac's "Hail Mary"
        && wonder what Abigail is doing now.
    } else if ( It's Tuesday || Thursday ){
        go to the computer lab
        && learn about computers
        && Abigail
        && Ms. Delaney
        && Emmy
        because no one else
        understands computers
        like we do.
    }
}
```

Been Fooled by September

This morning
as I walk up a hill
to take a bus
to the train
to another hill
to school
I realize my legs aren't shaking
and my lungs aren't gasping
as much as they used to.
And as I listen to my music
I see
through a gap in the clouds
the sun.

String

On Friday Ms. Delaney says
that when we put lots of characters together
also known as chars
we get a String.

I know String.
I recognize it
from my song.

I play it back to myself
and stop on a single word.

public
static
void
main . . .

String.

Ms. Delaney said that one day
we will learn what each word means
every single one
and for String
today is that day.

```
String =
```

String: A sequence of characters between two quotation marks. A String is treated literally, as the text between the quotes.

    For example,
```
"Hello, World!"
"Hello, Emmy!"
```

Unison

Ms. Delaney tells us to partner up.

My heart thumps
like a bass drum
as I look over
at Abigail

who is looking right back at me.

The musical girl
the back-to-class girl
the braids-in-her-hair-and-smile-on-her-face
Abigail
whose fun fact is that she is a Tetris champion
and has been singing since she was a toddler
with the San Francisco Children's Choir
and that she wants to be
the head of a Fortune 500 tech company
by the time she is 25

is looking at me
and at the exact same time
we both say {
    "Partner?"
}

What I Hear from Across the Room

Francis makes
an eye roll of a noise
and looks over at me
and my new partner {
    "Of course *they* are together."
}

I don't understand why
he said *they*
like it's a swear word

but Abigail nudges me
and we smile
a secret-sharing smile
and in my head
we shine red like **allegro
fortissimo**
the flourish of two electric violins.

Maybe Francis is the one
who doesn't belong.

Variables

Sometimes when you program
you want to tuck something away
and save it for later.
And so you give it a name
or a variable
so that you can call on it
when you need it most.

Abigail and I share the keyboard
making up variables
row by row {

```
String name = "Emmy";
String name2 = "Abigail";
int emmyAge = 12;
int abigailAge = 11;
String emmyDogName = "Jeopardy";
String abigailFavWord = "Wimbledon";
String emmyFavWord = "Pizzicato";
int abigailMeaningOfLife = 42;
String emmyFavMovie = "Howl's Moving Castle";
String abigailVoicePart = "alto";
int abigailNumberOfBrothers = 3;
int emmyNumberOfSiblings = 0;
String abigailFavBrother = "They're all dumb";
```
}

Storing Away

I close my eyes
take a breath

so that I have a chance
to give this feeling
this laughter
this joy
a variable
for when I need it most.

friend.

Etude

When I was three years old
Dad tried to teach me how to play piano
for the first time.

During our lessons
he would put his hand on mine
my fingertips stretching to meet his
and together
we'd play.

We would play and laugh and sing along
until his hands would leave mine.
Then my fingers would turn to french fries.
Stiff and stale.

That was when I first knew
my fingers didn't have any music in them.

But today
with Abigail
and our keyboards *clickety-clack*-ing
in two-part harmony
I wonder
if maybe
I was wrong.

Emmy and Abigail: An Actual Duet

"What if we try—"

"How about we—"

"Is this right?"

"Hmmmmm."

"I have an idea!"

"Oooh, that looks good."

"Is it working?"

"Oh! Let's try this!"

"Hmmmmm."

"How about—"

"Good idea!"

"Press the button and . . ."

"YES!"

Yes

After class
Abigail catches me
says {
    "I just got a raspberry pi
    as a birthday present
    from my parents.

    If you wanted to
    you could come over on Saturday
    after my choir practice
    and we could figure out how it works?"
}

And while I'm not sure
what there is to figure out
about a raspberry pie
I don't even need to think about it
before I say {
    "Yes!"
}

Dynamic

As it turns out
a raspberry pi
isn't a dessert at all
though there is leftover birthday cake.
Funfetti.
My favorite.

A raspberry pi
is a computer.

Abigail says it's sort of like what you'd find
if you cracked open a laptop
and then squished it all together
so small it can nuzzle in the palm of your hand.

But she says even though it's small
it's powerful.
All we need are some LED lights
a voice box
a resistor
a few cables
and the help of Abigail's brother Marcus
and we can program the raspberry pi
so the lights dance

to the sound
of our voices.

We shout
and the lights flash bright.
We whisper
and they flicker like a candle.
Like an orchestra responding to a conductor
the lights
listen
and I wonder
if the lights can do so much
with just shouts and whispers
what would they do
with music?

Global Variables

Sometimes `variables` last
and last
and
l   a   s   t.

You save them at the top of your program
so that anyone can use them.

There are other things
that I wish could
l   a   s   t
so I save them {

    Debugging with Abigail and her brother as we try to
    figure out why our code isn't working.

    Stifling our laughter at her little brother Jerome when he
    tries to burp the alphabet during dinner.

    Hugging goodbye, and promising we'll do this again
    soon.

    Going home Saturday night and telling Mom and Dad
    about how happy I am to have made a new friend.

}

Semicolon

The `semicolon` is the period at the end of a line—
of code.

It's the space between one perfect moment;

< 138 >

and whatever comes next.

Abigail Is Sick

and I may puke too.

I know as soon as homeroom
that she won't be in class.

The choir girls say she's sick
from across the room
but what I don't anticipate
is Ms. Delaney being gone
too.

Solo: Remix

The substitute says
that Ms. Delaney
had a last-minute doctor appointment
and he's filling in today
but she'll be back tomorrow.

But I don't care why they're not here.
All I care about
is that I don't like being by myself.
I don't like not being partnered.
I don't like being the only girl in the room.
I don't like how Francis
who had started to
disappear
when I was with Abigail
now feels bigger
and **bolder**
and ten times worse
than ever before.

Freeze

The substitute asks me a question and I

How can I speak
when all I can hear is
Francis
whispering . . .
                    . . . something

whisper whisper you whisper whisper whisper whisper
whisper whisper whisper don't whisper whisper whisper
whisper belong whisper whisper whisper in whisper whisper
whisper whisper computer whisper whisper class whisper

Stuck in My Head

I play back Abigail's words

> *Francis is a jerk (dee-dee-dee-dee-dee)*

but they scramble

> *Francis is right (doo-doo-doo-doo-doo)*

and without her next to me

> *He hates you (dah-dah-dah-dah-dah)*

it's like I'm back on stage

> *Only you (dum-dee-dum-dee-dum)*

mind going blank

> *No one else (you-oh-you-oh-you)*

and even though I know he's wrong

> *Don't belong (don't belong don't belong)*

without Abigail and Ms. Delaney

> *Don't belong (don't belong don't belong)*

I've never been more sure that Francis is right.

I don't belong here.

Goodbye, Emmy

String emmy = "don't belong don't belong
don't belong not here not there not anywhere
don't belong don't belong don't belong he's
right been right all along don't belong don't
belong don't belong head cock eye squint mouth
twist don't belong don't belong don't belong
ugly piano ugly piano ugly piano don't belong
don't belong don't belong head fuzzy vision
spotty ·fingers tingly stand up leave class don't
come back don't belong don't belong don't
belong";

The Girl Under the Stairs

The next day
Abigail still isn't in homeroom.

I don't want to go to the computer lab for lunch.
Instead I want to sit
under the stairs
and listen to my song.
But I know that no matter how many times I listen
I'm not a little kid anymore
and there are some things
that even music
can't erase.

The You-Belong-Here Girl

When lunch has started and all the students
except me
are where they belong
a voice from down the hallway
reaches me {
    "Hello, Emmy!";
}

So says a girl
a hand-out sort of girl
a palm-to-the-sky-fingers-taut sort of girl
a no-longer-sick-today-back-to-school girl.

She says {
    "My mom said I could come in today
    after I slept a little later than usual.
    Why aren't you in the lab?";
}
that take-my-hand girl.

That {
    "What's wrong?";
} sort of girl.

That {
    "Why are you under the stairs?"
} sort of girl.

That {
    "Come back to the lab. Please?"
} sort of girl.

That maybe
just maybe
a friend
sort of girl.

Variables: Remix

String whatEmmySaysFromUnderTheStairs = **"Do you ever feel like no matter what you do you just don't belong anywhere?"**;

String pause = **"**

";

String whatAbigailSaysBack = **"Doesn't everybody?"**;

Do Belong

Two
girls.

Two different girls.

Don't-Belongs
who belong
we belong
girls.

Yes: Remix

When we get to the lab
Ms. Delaney isn't smiling.
Her skirt isn't swishing the carpet.
Even her hair looks less springy.

If I didn't know better
I would say she looks
worried
maybe even
scared.

                              Is this all because I didn't show up?
She asks {
    "Are you okay?";
    "Did something happen yesterday with the substitute?";
    "Did something happen yesterday with Francis?";
}
And maybe it's because she's worried
and maybe it's because she noticed
and maybe it's because
it's just the three of us
that I feel comfortable enough
safe enough
to say {
    "Yes.";
}

One of the Above

I tell Ms. Delaney what happened
about the whispers
and the faces
and the squirms
and the SNORTs
and as I say it
it feels small
unimportant
like I maybe even imagined it.

But Ms. Delaney says {
    "It's one thing
     for him to treat me this way
     and another thing
     for him to do it to you.

     I'm going to come up with a plan.
     And in the meantime
     how do you want to spend the rest of this period?";
}
I look at Abigail
who looks at me
and I say {
    "Let's write some code!";
}

Blink

and you miss it.

The next day in class
Ms. Delaney takes
Francis's sweater
from around his swivel chair
and folds it up neatly
on her desk.

The Plan

I like it in the computer lab
just me and Abigail and Ms. Delaney.

We're good together.

But when the clock strikes 12:45
she says {
   "Look at the time!
    Our visitor should be arriving shortly.";
}

She points to a table
where there is a sweater
Francis's
folded up on a table
under a sign {
   "Lost and Found";
}

And something in Ms. Delaney's expression
makes me feel like maybe
Francis is going to find
more than just his sweater.

The Girls That Belonged

I know Francis has walked in
because Ms. Delaney cuts herself off mid-
sentence and starts a new one {
    "Did you know
      that the first computers wore lipstick?";
}

Francis looks over
but we're playing along
and he's being played.

Ms. Delaney says {
    "They wore lipstick
      because the first computers
      were women.";
}

Francis slings his sweater over his shoulder
but he's circling the lab
like he might have forgotten something else.

Ms. Delaney says {
    "A lot of misguided people believe
      that girls don't belong in computer science
      and it hurts to love something so much

when the world wants you to believe
that it doesn't love you back.

But the older I get the funnier it becomes
because I know something they don't.
In the beginning
it was the BOYS that didn't belong.
While the men were off fighting in World War Two
the women stayed behind and computed.

Without the computers in lipstick
we wouldn't have `algorithms`
we would still be programming in binary
instead of languages that look and feel like English
and for all we know
maybe we would have never made it to the moon.";
}

Francis has found
whatever it was he wasn't looking for
and now he's out the door.

Ms. Delaney smiles her **fortissimo** smile
and says {
    "Anyone who thinks
    you don't belong here
    is just plain wrong.";
}

A Small Violin

The next day in class
Francis sits by himself.

He looks angry
-er than usual
like he still can't believe
this
is the elective he's stuck in
all semester long.

But I guess Ms. Delaney's plan worked
because he doesn't say anything to me
and avoids eye contact
even when I'm looking right at him
and by the time Abigail walks into class
and sits down next to me
I couldn't care less
about Francis.

While Loop

Today Ms. Delaney teaches us
about the magic of a `while` loop.

Abigail and me
me and Abigail
     we
revel in Francis's quiet.
We take up the space
he used to fill.

We laugh loud
and make mistakes
and use our `while` loop
to do silly things
like print our names
to infinity.
Over and over and over and over
and over
again—

Hello, Emmy! Hello, Abigail! Hello, Emmy! Hello, Abigail!
Hello, Emmy! Hello, Abigail! Hello, Emmy! Hello, Abigail!
Hello, Emmy! Hello, Abigail! Hello, Emmy! Hello Abigail!
Hello, Emmy! Hello, Abigail! Hello, Emmy! Hello, Abigail!
Hello, Emmy! Hello, Abigail! Hello, Emmy! Hello, Abigail!
Hello, Emmy! Hello, Abigail! Hello, Emmy! Hello Abigail!
Hello, Emmy! Hello, Abigail! Hello, Emmy! Hello, Abigail!
Hello, Emmy! Hello, Abigail! Hello, Emmy! Hello, Abigail!
Hello, Emmy! Hello, Abigail! Hello, Emmy! Hello Abigail!
Hello, Emmy! Hello, Abigail! Hello, Emmy! Hello, Abigail!
Hello, Emmy! Hello, Abigail! Hello, Emmy! Hello, Ab—

—until
we are laughing so hard
that Ms. Delaney has to come over
and remind us that there are others
trying to focus on their own work
before we're willing
to let our `while` loop end.

Termination

`while` loops end
when their condition is no longer satisfied.

`while` (The time is between 11:15 && 11:59 a.m.) {
    learn to program;
    sit next to Abigail;
    watch my computer greet me
        over and over and over and over;
    and most importantly
    laugh;
    but don't get too used to it because
    all
    good
    things
    must
}

terminate.

12:01 p.m.

Instead of goodbye
Abigail says {
    "Hello, Emmy!";
}
and I laugh
at our first inside joke.
We walk out of the classroom
smiles pulling at our jaws

but there are those voices again
calling from down the hall.
A chorus.
A Symphony Orchestra and Choir
of {
    "We're here to rescue you!";
}

I try
to bring Abigail back inside
the safety of our `while` loop.

But the condition is no longer `true`.

What I Hear from Down the Hall

"I still can't believe you ended up in this dumb class."

>   "Abigail, are you positive
>   you signed up for music?"

>   "If the choir altos
>   are the ones auditioning
>   then the Honey Bees aren't going to be any good."

"I swear
they're so bad it almost makes me wish
I had taken cooking."

>   "Oh, come on, we're not that bad."

"Everything will be fine
if Abigail can just make it through
the audition!"

>   "If anyone can do it
>   without even being in the regular choir
>   it's Abigail."

>   "Yeah!
>   I'm sure you can still get in, Abs!"

"But you should keep trying to switch
just in case."

>   "Yeah!
>   I hate thinking of you in a class
>   with all these weirdos."

What I Don't Hear . . .

. . . is Abigail saying anything at all.

Small Steps

Today I try something

BIG.

I listen to my music
and eat my lunch
at a table
in the cafeteria
where maybe I'm starting to feel like
I belong

just a little.

Why did no one tell me
that in San Francisco
October
is when the sun starts to shine?

Disappear

There's music in me.
I can feel it again

sur

```
          m               g
      u       p       n
  j               i
```

cha-
    cha-
        chaing

I know what happens when I sit at the bench
but Mom's still at work
and Dad's busy with dinner
so I do it anyway.

Even though my fingers
won't do what I say
sometimes I let that disappear
and enjoy the feeling
of just being near
Dad's ugly yellow piano.

Downbeat

Mom comes in late
after dinner
for the third night in a row.

Dad has saved her slice of pizza
her bowl of matzo ball soup
her steak and eggs

but every day it's cold.

Mom asks how my day was
and I ask about hers.

We trade *fine*s
but I'm starting to believe hers less and less
even as I believe mine
more and more.

Whole Rest: Remix

This is the part of the day when I used to practice piano.

But now Dad is cleaning the kitchen
and Mom is eating reheated steak and eggs
while working from the couch
I sit at the keyboard
and try to make my computer
sing.

I code and code and code
and whatever I type
the computer listens.

Now it's eight o'clock
and the house is quiet
except for my fingers
*tap-tap-tap*ping on the keys.

I wonder if Mom or Dad would understand
that even though
they call it computer *science*
to me
it feels like
what I always wanted it to feel like
when I played music.

Duo + 1

Abigail and I
me and Abigail
walk into the computer lab on Tuesday at lunch.

But Ms. Delaney isn't alone.

She is re-explaining `variables`
to Iain
waving her hands around
like she's conducting a symphony.

But he's frustrated.
You can tell
because
in his double-bass voice
he makes a joke {
    "Why did you leave your fancy job
     to come teach idiots
     like me?";
}

Ms. Delaney smiles
a cherry-red smile
but one that isn't so **allegro**
fortissimo

vivace

and definitely not `boolean`.

She says {

    "The absolute LAST thing

    that you are

    in the whole entire world

    is an idiot.";

}

Ms. Delaney's Fairy Tale

Once upon a time there was a magical land where people could come together to work, learn, and change the world. The magical land was a company, but it was also a palace. They had sand pits, ball pits, and staticky slides, rooms full of arcade games, and the most delicious food you've ever tasted in your life.

Everyone was happy, deliriously so, and couldn't think of anywhere else they would rather be. And for a while Ms. Delaney was happy there too. She liked her work and she liked the people she worked with, and she *loved* changing the world.

But sometimes the best dungeons are the ones that look like palaces.

Over time Ms. Delaney started to notice the golden chains clanking on her wrists. The twine stringing up the smiles of everyone around her. The stone-thick walls meant for more than just keeping others out.

One day she had a reason to leave the castle, and once she was gone she couldn't bring herself to go back.

Before she knew it, she was gone for good.

And now she can live happily ever after.

THE END

Trio

Iain is smart.
He asks good questions
and answers ours
in ways that make things stick {
    "`for` loops are just `while` loops
     dressed up for Halloween.";

    "Exclusive or is just like
     `or` minus `and`.";

    "Binary is just counting
     if you only had two fingers.";
}

Iain is like the part of Beethoven's Fifth Symphony
just when it's getting dark and loud
when the piccolos float in
all bright and shiny and happy.

I guess it's okay
if lunch periods are not a duet anymore.

You can't have a symphony
with just two people.

Bracket Bracket

On Wednesday Ms. Delaney teaches about lists
and I understand
not one
but two
new words in my song.

public
static
void
main
String

Bracket Bracket.

[]

Building blocks can be small
like boolean
and String
and int
but put a few together and you get
something bigger.
An array.
A list.
Bracket Bracket.

[ ] =

[ ]: Notation used to declare that a variable is meant to be an array, or list, of that object type.

For example,

```
String[] msDelaneysClass = new String[] {
    "Emmy",
    "Abigail",
    "Iain",
    "Drake",
    "Evan"
};

String[] potentialFunFacts = new String[] {
    "Mom says that when I graduate middle school
    they'll buy me a new laptop and then I can
    take this one apart to see what's inside.",
    "Dad just picked up two new private lesson
    clients!",
    "That video of me and Jeopardy waltzing is
    up to five thousand views."
};
```

Errors

When we try to run our code
it spits out
an error.

Angry red text
letting us know
that something went wrong.

Ms. Delaney says {
   "My favorite!
    A mystery to be solved!"
}

Did we add two things together that aren't numbers?
Or try to print something that isn't a `String`?
Did we put something inside an `if` that isn't a `boolean`?
Or did we spell something wrong?

Or maybe it's a bigger error than all that.
Maybe we misunderstood something.

Ms. Delaney says {
   "Errors are great
    because the computer is doing my job for me
    pointing out where you are still confused.

And that's okay
because programming is hard
and errors are meant to help you.
But if you can't figure it out
you can always ask me!";
}

When she says it like that
errors don't seem that bad.
They're just another mystery
meant to be solved
by the dynamic debugging duo
that is
Emmy and Abigail.

The Dynamic Debugging Duet

Abigail and I are
unstoppable.
We finish our work early

single

Write a program
that prints out
all the even numbers
less than 100.

Write a program
that prints out
all the three-letter words
that contain either an A

but not both.

Together

He doesn't matter when we're
together.

Emmy and I are
unstoppable.

every

day.

Write a program
that plays an alarm bell
every hour on the hour.

or an E

Done, done, and done
with seven minutes left.
Together
we ignore Francis.

together.

Girls

When Abigail laughs
she laughs and laughs and laughs.
She laughs way down deep in her gut
like a tuba
or an alto sax.
So big you can't help but sing along.

When Abigail laughs
her mouth opens wide
white teeth standing stark against her skin
like piano keys.

When Abigail laughs
I do too.

And then she laughs harder
just because I'm laughing
and suddenly our jaws are hurting
and before I know it
Abigail whispers in my ear {
    "Don't tell anyone
        but I think you're my best friend.";
}

A Chord, Resolving

Sometimes I need to be reminded to walk Jeopardy.
Sometimes I go to my room
while Dad practices piano.
Sometimes I'd rather code from my bedroom
than watch the Food Network in the living room.
Sometimes I'd rather message Abigail all day
than talk to those
who don't get computers
like us.

Mom laughs it off
with a cymbal crash
and a shuffle of papers
for her new job {
    "Hey, if it wasn't going to be music
     at least it's something
     that could one day make her money!";
}

But that isn't it at all.

When I'm programming
it feels like what it sounds like
when Dad plays the final **chords**
of a Mozart sonata.

Like when Mom sings
"Con onor muore"
the final number in *Madame Butterfly*.
It's like everything is resolving itself
and in its proper place
after a l-o-o-o-o-o-o-o-o-o-o-o-o-o-o-o-o-o-o-o-o-o-o-o-o-o-o-o-
o-o-o-o-o-o-o-o-o-o-o-o-o-o-o-o-o-o-o-o-o-o-ng journey.

And when my brain is working this hard
sometimes I forget
that I ever felt like
I didn't
belong.

Methods

A `variable` by itself is nice
but it's even nicer
when it does something.
And so we learn about `methods`.

`Methods` can be commands that do something {

```
    circle.draw();
    alarmBellSoundClip.start();
    System.out.println("Hello, World!");
}
```

or questions that return something {

```
    int squareRoot = Math.sqrt(16);
    boolean isEmmyThere = "Hello, Emmy!".contains("Emmy!");
    String bestFriends = "Emmy and".append("Abigail");
}
```

And the best part is
once you define a `method`
you can call it over and over and over again.

```
void printFriends() {
    System.out.println("Emmy and Abigail");
}
```

```
printFriends();
printFriends();
printFriends();
```

Void

public
static

void

void sounds like black holes
bottomless pits
light getting stuck
because the night is too thick.

But Ms. Delaney says that even though void sounds scary
there's nothing bad about it.
void means the method is a command
not a question
and we shouldn't expect it to respond
after we call it {
    "Like when Evan is too busy reading his phone
     to pay attention to class!";
}
Everyone laughs
even Evan
who puts his phone back in his pocket
and I store away the knowledge
of void
in its very own variable.

```
void =
```

Void: A keyword used to signify that a method does something when it's run, but does not return a value. Used in contrast to a method that returns a value when called.

For example,
```
evan.putYourPhoneAway();
abigail.lookAtMeInThatWayWhenWeAreInOnTheSameJoke();
emmy.smile();
emmy.smile();
emmy.smile();
```

Raspberry

This weekend
I go to Abigail's house again
after her choir rehearsal
to test out a robotics kit she got
for her raspberry pi.

Dad drives me
because Mom is on the phone with her boss
and we listen to Stevie Wonder
on repeat
the whole way over.

I guess it gets stuck in my head
because as soon as Abigail answers the door
she asks {
    "What's that you're singing?";
}

I can feel my face
turn the color of
raspberry.

I didn't realize I was singing
and I **don't**
sing in public.

Not after what happened last time.

But when I respond
and say {
   "'Sir Duke'";
}
Abigail says {
   "Oh, I know that one!
    I sang the solo in that once
    in SFCC!";
}
and right there in her foyer
she starts singing.

Abigail

Abigail's voice
is
incredible.

It sounds like . . .

Well
I don't think I've ever
heard anything like it before

but it tastes
like salted caramel

smells
like Wisconsin summertime

feels
like cuddling with Jeopardy on the couch

but when I tell her this
Abigail's smile flips
and it looks like maybe
for Abigail
singing isn't quite
boolean.

Abigail's Fairy Tale

Once upon a time there was a princess with braided hair and a voice so beautiful that she could make a statue smile. Everyone who heard the princess sing would become happy, even if they didn't know why.

And so the princess sang.

She sang in choirs, talent shows, and sometimes even competitions. She made friends with other princesses who also sang, but everyone knew the princess in braids had the most beautiful voice in the land.

But the princess had a secret. Her singing made everyone else a whole lot happier than it made her. The princess preferred robots and wires and booleans and Java, and if she had it her way, she would only sing in the royal shower.

But the princess's singing made everyone else so happy that she continued to do it. Until one day, she made a choice. Instead of spending one more minute singing, she would spend her time learning about what she really loved: robots and wires and booleans and Java.

And now she can live happily ever after.

THE END

What You Hate

I guess I understand
what Abigail's saying.
If you don't love something
is it even worth doing?

I spend the day on Abigail's living room floor
building a robot with my friend.

It's cool
I guess.
He can walk
and respond to our voices.
We even name him Bob
because he kind of looks like a Bob.

But I can't help thinking that it doesn't seem fair.

I spent so many years
wishing
for a voice like hers
and here she is
playing with wires

wasting it.

What If?: Remix

```
if ( I had Abigail's voice )  {
    I would sing every chance I got;
}


if ( I had Abigail's voice )  {
    the music in me would always have a place to go;
}


if ( I had Abigail's voice )  {
    no one would look at me with an ugly piano face;
}


if ( I had Abigail's voice )  {
    I wouldn't be spending my time
        sitting on my living room floor
        making robots;
}


if ( I had Abigail's voice )  {
    I would always know where I belonged
        and not just
        when I'm in
        the computer lab;
}
```

Moving Out

Ms. Delaney is proud
of how quickly we learned `methods`.
And I can tell that she means it
because her smile is even brighter
than usual.

And so
on Monday
she says
now that we have mastered the art
of `methods`
we should use them to break

                    our

             code

                           up

so that it's easier to read.

But I like it when it's all together.
When it sits
safe and snug
inside the main `method`
with its friends
where it should be.

Main

When we move our code out of main
I see it for what it is.

public
static
void

main.

main is just a method name
like smile()
or putYourPhoneAway()
or lookAtMeInThatWayWhenWeAreInOnTheSameJoke()
but it's special
because the computer knows to look for it.

main is like when Abigail walks into a room
and I hear a door swing open
and there's nothing special about the swing
but I know it's her
because I'm keeping my ears open.

When I tell Abigail this
she says they shouldn't have named it main.
They should have named it best.

`main =`

Main: A reserved word in Java. When asked to run a program, the virtual machine will search for the method called `main` and run the code that sits inside it.

The Cafeteria: Remix

The cafeteria feels like a program
where our computer class divides back up
into their individual methods.

```
drakeAndFrancis() {
    sit with the Minecraft boys;
    eat pizza;
    drink Coke Zero;
    argue about which version of CIV is superior;
}

evan() {
    sit with the skaters;
    draw tattoos on each other's arms;
    sneak off campus for lunch
        even though we aren't allowed
        until eighth grade;
}

iain() {
    sit with the track team;
    flirt with the girls' basketball team
        —Go Bumblebees!;
    arm wrestle;
}
```

```
abigail() {
    sit with Rebecca and Angel and Divya;
    eat spaghetti night leftovers;
    talk about the SFCC
            and the upcoming auditions for the Honey Bees;
}
```

I sit alone
thinking about how it's better when we're all together
in `main`
even if it can be a bit messy.

Separate Methods

Sometimes I wonder what they're talking about
Abigail and her friends
at their cafeteria table
    but it must be funny
    because they're laughing so hard.
Sometimes I wonder if Abigail sees me here
listening to my music
by myself
    but she must not
    because she's never said hi.
Sometimes we pass by each other
when we leave for our next classes
and sometimes I even wave
    but I'm sure she hasn't seen me
    because she never waves back.
 And sometimes I wonder
 why I'm not allowed to tell anyone
 that she and I are best
 friends.

```
Emmy() {

        eat your weird grains;
        listen to your music;
        sit by yourself;
        miss being in the computer lab;
}
```

The Symphony

The computer lab
is the swishing and whirling of swivel chairs
on soft-carpet floors
like the glissando of a harp.
And the tick-a-tick of double clicking
over the clickety-clack of six keyboards.
It's the whispers of
"Well, I guess—"
"How about—"
"That means that—"
that mix and meld in three-quarter time.

And through it all
my heart beats along
boom-bah-dah
boom-bah-dah
boom
like it's the bass line
loud and proud
pounding

we be-long
we be-long
we be-long.

My Music

I'm the last one in the classroom
except for Ms. Delaney
packing my backpack
sl-o-o-o-o-o-o-o-o-o-o-o-o-o-o-o-o-o-o-w
when Ms. Delaney asks {
    "What's that you're singing?";
}

Something must have gotten into me lately
because I am singing again
without realizing it
and while normally
the thought of singing out loud
would make my face go
raspberry
this time I allow myself
to repeat
my song {
    "PUB-lic
    STAT-ic
    void, main, string.
    BRACK-et
    BRACK-et
    ARGS!";
}

Shared Music

Ms. Delaney laughs so hard
at first I think
she's teasing
and my head threatens
to go fuzzy.
But I should have known better
because when she wipes her eyes
she says {
    "That's how I sing it too!";
}

Dolce

Dad plays Chopin tonight.
Sweet.
Just like the cinnamon apple tart
that sits cooling
on our countertop.

Randomness

I'm excited for class today
like I am every day
until Ms. Delaney says {
   "Today
     we're going to play with randomness.
     Practice our lists a bit
     and writing `methods`
     by building a partner generator.

     If your input is a class of people
     I want you
     to generate a random set of partnerships.

     And to test this
     I'm assigning your partners today
     with the program that I wrote using randomness.";
}
Ms. Delaney runs her own program
and our class is
sracmbeld.
Abigail is with Drake
and Iain is with Evan.
I should have guessed
that randomness would put me with
Francis.

Bright Side

There is some consolation
in knowing that Francis
looks just as mad about this
as I am.

Emmy and Francis: A Duet, If You Can Call It That

"Can I try something?"

"You're not going to do it right."

"But I have an idea—"

"Stop talking and let me think!"

"What about—"

"Shut up!"

"Okay . . . fine . . ."

"Ugh!"

". . ."

"Why won't this work?"

". . ."

"Stupid computer!"

"Can I try my idea?"

"ARGH!"

Francis stands up
and then
SLAM!

SLAM!

Francis is standing
over a cockeyed
upside-down
backside-front
keyboard
cable twisted
after he
SLAMMED
it on the desk.

Ms. Delaney says {
   "Francis!
    We   do   not
    treat computers that way.
    Go out in the hallway
    and I will be out there in a minute
    to talk to you.";
}

But Ms. Delaney
didn't need to tell him
to go anywhere
because the door is
SLAMMING
before she can finish her sentence.

4'33": Remix

The room is silent
while Ms. Delaney talks to Francis in the hall.

Silent enough
that if I listen
as hard as I can
I can hear him talking.

Francis's Fairy Tale

Once upon a time there was a wizard with computers. His powers were so strong that it was said that he could build anything—anything at all!—just by tapping on a keyboard.

One day the wizard had a daughter, and she wanted to be a wizard too. But the wizard had inherited his powers from his father, and he refused to pass his own powers down to anyone except a son.

So the wizard's daughter was left to her own devices. She practiced incantations in the basement, read dusty scrolls beneath her blankets, and by the time the wizard did have a son, the wizard's daughter was as good a wizard as any twelve-year-old child could be.

As the years went by, the wizard's daughter made her own wizarding way, her powers growing and growing until they rivaled even those of her father. Meanwhile, the wizard pushed his son that much harder so he could be better than the daughter who never should have been a wizard at all.

And now the wizard's son—Francis—has no choice but to be the greatest wizard on earth.

And he *will* live happily ever after.

THE END

Not Quite Boolean

When I leave the classroom
Francis tells me he's sorry.

His voice sounds wobbly
like a violin with too much vibrato
and his eyes look as red
as Ms. Delaney's lipstick.

I guess that's why I say {
   "That's okay.";
} even though
I'm not sure that it is.

Forgiveness
is the least boolean thing
in the entire world.

Avoiding

For the rest of the day
whenever I see Francis coming

he turns

the corner.

Punch Cards

It's nice to be in computer club today
no Francis in sight.
And what we learn about today is so cool
that I almost forget about yesterday.

Ms. Delaney says {
    "Did you know that computers used to be so big
    that just one could fill up our whole classroom?
    That they didn't have screens back then
    and when you wrote a program
    you couldn't write it in words.
    If you think
    public
    static
    void
    main
    String
    bracket
    bracket
    args
    takes a long time to type out
    try writing our programs in a language called
    Fortran.";
}

< 207 >

Ms. Delaney pulls out a thick sheet of paper.
It looks like a plane ticket
if a plane ticket
was covered in numbers
and attacked by a three-hole punch.

She says {
    "This is a punch card.";
}

Abigail takes it from Ms. Delaney
runs her fingers over it
and wouldn't you know it?
Letter by letter
she starts to *read*.

```
String[] whatAbigailReads =

"P
R
O
G
R
A
M
H
E
L
L
O
W
O
R
L
D";
```

Seriously, is there anything she can't do?

```java
String[] itemsOnMsDelaneysDesk =

{
    "A figurine of a robot dressed like Albert
    Einstein",

    "A glass cube engraved with Congratulations
    for a patent in computer security",

    "A Polaroid of six smiling faces pointing to
    a bowl of nachos",

    "A framed ticket to a Beatles concert signed
    by John Lennon",

    "A yoyo",

    "A tube of candy-apple red lipstick",

    "A Polaroid of a baby wrapped in a purple
    blanket",

    "A stack of punch cards that somehow Abigail
    can read"
};
```

Emmy and Abigail: The Dyn--

Abigail and I
leave the computer lab
together.

single

We talk about while loops

and how Abigail's brother
sounds like a walrus
when he snores.

and everything

are best

friends

Emmy and I
leave the computer lab
together.
Every

day.

void methods

and how my brother
sounds like a walrus
when he snores.

We'll talk about anything

because we

fr-

"We're here to rescue you!"

While Loop: Remix

```
while ( In the computer lab )  {
    you and Abigail are friends;
}
```


I guess all good things
really do terminate.

Diminished Fifth

I wonder what they're talking about
Abigail and her friends
at their cafeteria table

           because every day Abigail's laughs get
           softer.
And ever since that time at her house
when I heard her sing
I know she sees me here
listening to my music
by myself

           because she can't help but look at me.
And today when we pass by each other
when the bell rings
as we're off to our next classes
I accidentally
on purpose
give her a half wave

                    which she returns
                    when her friends round

the corner.

Off-Key

On Saturday
I get a call from Abigail.

She ordered a motion detector
for the raspberry pi
and it just arrived in the mail.
Would I want to come over
and test it out?

A few weeks ago
I wouldn't have even had to think
but today
I pause.

I'm the only one who knows
how Abigail feels about her voice.

I'm the only one who knows
how much Abigail loves computers.

She says I'm her best friend
but if that's true
why am I still
a secret?

I know it's not easy
making new friends
or keeping old ones
but how can I go to her house
and pretend everything is normal
when everything inside me feels
out of tune?

So I say {
    "Thanks but I have plans already.";
}
and hang up.

Ms. Delaney's Fairy Tale: Remix

When Ms. Delaney talks about
her old projects
at her old job
her voice sounds like Mom's
when she talks about opera.
Soft and nostalgic
like Corelli's **Adagio**
from his *Christmas Concerto.*

So when Iain raises his hand and asks {
   "If your old job was so great
    then why did you leave?";
}

Ms. Delaney's voice trips
as if over a wrong note in a **fugue**.

But she covers it up
with a clearing cough
and takes a moment of white space
before talking. {
   "I never used to wear dresses at my old job.
   No skirts
   lipstick
   high-heeled shoes.

I didn't want to stick out.
Be too girly.
Or 'unprofessional.'
But somewhere along the line
I got sick of not being myself.
Plus something happened
that made me realize how little time we have
and that I shouldn't waste it
being just half
of who I am.";
}

I look at Abigail
and she looks at the floor
as if maybe Ms. Delaney
has struck a **chord**.

Augmented Fifth

Ms. Delaney is gone on Tuesday
for another doctor appointment
but this time
at lunchtime
I don't go to my own table.

I'm sick of it.
Sitting alone
listening to my music
while Abigail has everything.
The voice
      the friends
            the secret second life
                  as a computer genius.

There's no reason
I shouldn't have it
too.

So today
I find
the string quartet {
      "Can I sit with you?";
}

Cafeteria Logic

```
String[] thingsThatAreTrue = new String[] {
    "Emmy, these are my friends. Divya, Rebecca,
     and Angel.",
    "We've been friends since preschool when
     we all joined our afterschool choir at the
     same time.",
    "Emmy is in my computer class."
};


String[] thingsThatAreFalse = new String[] {
    "Computer class would be awful if it weren't
     for Emmy.",
    "Emmy is also with me at music theory for
     Tuesday and Thursday lunch.",
    "Our music theory teacher is sick today
     which is why we're in the cafeteria."
};


String[] thingsThatAreNotQuiteBoolean = new String[] {
    "Hi, Emmy.",
    "Nice to meet you, Emmy.",
    "Hey."
};
```

Presto

The conversation whizzes
like Chopin's *Fantaisie-Impromptu* {
    "The auditions are—";
    "Ms. Sinclair said—";
    "Sing from your—";
}

It's hard to find white space
in the conversation
and whenever I take a breath—
The moment has passed {
    "The altos—";
    "We should ask—";
    "Practice will be—";
}

But what would I say anyway?
These are the *musician* girls
and I already decided
I am not a musician.

Besides
my new favorite conversation topics
    computers && Java && Ms. Delaney
are off-limits.

Attempted Duet No. 6

When the bell rings
everyone says goodbye
in their own way {
    "See you at rehearsal tonight!";
    "Have fun with you-know-who next period.";
    "Can we practice *Messiah* in the car?";
}

So in the noise
I add in our inside joke
our own music {
    "Hello, Abigail.";
}

The Latest Schedule

```
if ( It's fourth period )  {
    if ( It's Monday || Wednesday || Friday )  {
        have computer class
            just like normal;
    } else if ( It's Tuesday || Thursday )  {
        go to the computer lab;
        eat your whole lunch;
        learn about everything {
            Abigail
            && Iain
            && Ms. Delaney
            && Emmy;
        }
    }
} else if ( It's Monday || Wednesday || Friday )  {
    see Iain sitting with the track team;
    see Drake && Francis sitting with the Minecraft boys;
    see Evan sitting with the skaters;
    find Abigail's table;
    sit with Angel && Divya && Rebecca && Abigail;
    force down what you can of your lunch;
    pretend you belong;
}
```

Atonal Music

Drake shows up the next Thursday at lunch.

He says {
    "Don't look so surprised.
     Ms. Delaney said you were talking about C++ today.";
}

C++
is the name of another computer language
but I don't think I like it very much.

When I hear the name Java
it makes me want to curl up
in front of the fireplace

but when I hear C++
I think about wires
cold metal
steely assembly lines.

But I guess it's like how Dad's been playing
that new piece.
The one that used to sound like
cracking knuckles
but now sounds like something more.

It's atonal
and just takes some practice to understand.

I wonder if Drake would like atonal music
because when Ms. Delaney pulls up her code
I can't see how it all comes together
and maybe someday I will
but Drake must see it
because he melts into himself
like he really is curled up by the fire.

Digital Art

Ms. Delaney says {
    "You all know that Java isn't
    the only programming language.
    And though it's wonderful for high-level learning
    Android development
    and simple user interfaces
    there are other languages out there
    that are better for other projects.
    So I want to show you something I built in C++.";
}

The code looks messy.
The symbols don't make sense.
And while I can recognize some words
it's written using a different IDE
so even the familiar looks wrong.

Ms. Delaney continues {
    "Last night I finished a project
    and I wanted to show you
    because while coding is fun
    to me
    it's not the ultimate goal.
    We all program for different reasons.
    To save lives

        to have fun
        to find a need and fill it
        to challenge ourselves
        to make something out of nothing.
        Code is a form of expression
        just like any other.

        And for me
        code is art.";
}

She clicks a button
and there it is
glowing faintly purple on the computer screen
something beautiful
out of the chaos.

Hidden Lessons: Remix

When class is over
and everyone has packed their bags
I hang back {
    "Ms. Delaney?
    Does the art have to be visual?";
}

Ms. Delaney spins in her swivel chair
like she's doing a pirouette. {
    "I'm not sure what you mean.";
}

I think about the LED lights
that I made with Abigail all those weeks ago
flashing
dancing
and point to the purple picture
still on her computer screen. {
    "I mean
    can you use computers
    to make
    music?";
}

Ms. Delaney looks at the clock
then looks at me
then back at the clock.

Then she clicks over to her email
and types something that I'm too polite to read
before clicking back to the coding window. {
   "I was supposed to go to a concert tonight
    but this is FAR more important.";
}

4:00 p.m.

I don't think it's a coincidence
that `algorithm`
has inside it
a little "rhythm."

`Algorithms` are formulas
patterns programmed into a computer
and Ms. Delaney teaches me how to write one
that generates music.

It sounds like hopping
like crickets chirping
and sparrows singing.

We tweak some numbers and it sounds like marching
like thunder rolling
and rain pounding.

We tweak it again and it sounds like swimming
and again and it sounds like clapping
and again and it sounds like rays of sunlight

For the first time
I know there's music
in me.

Digital Music

The music

        m
    u   p
j   s

cha-
    cha-
        chas

And as I sit in a swivel chair
next to Ms. Delaney
with my hands on the keys

I feel like
a musician.

```
String[] whyMsDelaneyLeftHerJob =

{

    "She didn't really quit; she was fired
    because she stole government secrets.",

    "A great-aunt she didn't know she had sud-
    denly died and left her a billion dollars.",

    "Her boss wanted her to kill someone and
    she couldn't bring herself to do it.",

    "The commute was too long.",

    "She wanted to pursue her career as a country-
    western singer, but she got laryngitis, so
    she decided to teach instead.",

    "She never worked at a big tech company
    at all—she's really a spy and wants our
    help to crack a secret code sent to us by
    aliens.",

    "Or maybe there's nothing to hide, and she
    just one day woke up and realized that she
    didn't like it anymore."

};
```

But Abigail and I don't have time
to choose the best one
before her friends show up
and Abigail changes
threads— {
    "You crushed your solo audition on Saturday!";
}

Lento

If Ms. Delaney is our conductor
then today we are playing a Mozart **requiem**.

The lights are low in the room
which Ms. Delaney says
is because her eyes are hurting.

She was a little late today
which she says is because
she had a meeting with the principal.

But what really worries me
is that her hands don't do somersaults
they lie flat
like hands.

She seems distracted by something
though I don't understand what
and so it's no surprise
that even though today is a class day
and not a club day
Ms. Delaney pulls up a chair
and talks to us.

Artificial Intelligence

Ms. Delaney says {
    "Some people think
    it may be possible
    to upload your brain into a computer.";
}

Abigail laughs. {
    "That's ridiculous.
    You wouldn't have a body.";
}

But it doesn't sound so ridiculous to me.
I say {
    "You'd be a soul.";
}

Ms. Delaney nods, hands still quiet. {
    "Some people believe consciousness
    can fit on a thumb drive
    if we could only reduce it
    to ones and zeroes.

    Some people believe human brains
    are just computers

infinitely complex
but computers nonetheless.

Some people even believe that
if we separated the person
from the body
then we'd have the power
to create life
or even
to defy

death.";
}

Machine Learning

Ms. Delaney spends the rest of the period
showing us examples
of people who are trying to crack the code
to human life.

She asks us
What makes a human mind?
If a machine analyzed our speech patterns
could it recreate our voice?

She talks about the Turing test
which asks
How would we know
if we were talking to a robot?

She shows us machines
that you can talk to online
about the weather
or the news.
They can tell stories
make jokes
and sometimes even
laugh.

How do we know they're not people?

Everyone else thinks that last bit is funny
but I just can't stop thinking
about that one little D-word Ms. Delaney used
in the first few minutes of class
that no one else seemed to hear.

Thinking about it makes my stomach curl
like a sousaphone
and I wonder
if this is supposed to be
a casual conversation
then why does Ms. Delaney's voice
sound so sad?

White Space

My Tupperware full of spelt
and sesame seeds
rests on the table
while Angel && Divya && Rebecca && Abigail talk.

I've eaten most of my lunch
and maybe it's because I'm still thinking
about Ms. Delaney's lesson
or maybe it's because I'm so focused
on chewing
and chewing
and swallowing
that I find the white space
the breath
the pause
in the conversation.

> I'd say it was an accident
> but that would be `false`.

Not an Accident

Rebecca is talking
about a movie she saw last weekend {
    "Did you know there was a group of women
    in the basement of NASA
    doing all these big calculations on blackboards
    for the first space launch?";
}

And I know I don't have to say anything
but I'm
just
so
tired
of having a secret
of being a secret
of living a secret
that I say {
    "It's just like what Ms. Delaney says
    in our extra lunchtime computer classes.
    Remember, Abigail?";
}

Explain

Abigail's face
fades
and I slide
down in my seat
while she tries
to explain
why she lied
about where she goes
during lunch
on Tuesdays
and Thursdays.

```java
String[] whatAbigailSays =

{
    "I'm sorry I lied to you. That wasn't right.",

    "Yes...I mean...no...I didn't try to switch out.",

    "I should have told the truth.",

    "Well, maybe I don't want to audition for the
     Honey Bees.",

    "Or maybe I do! I don't know! Why do I need
     to decide right this second?",

    "Sometimes I wonder if I really like singing.",

    "You three will be fine if I don't make it in.",

    "I don't owe you anything!",

    "Wait!",

    "Don't leave!",

    "Wait!"
};
```

The Silent Treatment

When everyone is gone
Abigail gets up from the table
and without even looking at me
storms off.

I say {
   "I'm sorry.";
}
but she doesn't look back
even though I know she hears me.

Arguments

public
static
void
main
String
bracket
bracket . . .

args.

An argument is a fight.

An argument is what comes between two friends.

An argument is what Abigail and I are in right now.

But Ms. Delaney says {
    "An argument is a parameter.";
}

```
args =
```

Parameter: A parameter is a variable passed into a
method to be used as input. Also known as an argument.

Args: A default variable name for the parameter in the main
method.

   For example,
```
boolean willYouForgiveMeIf(String args);
```

```
boolean willYouForgiveMeIf(String args);
```

```
abigail.willYouForgiveMeIf(
    "I send you an apology email?");
abigail.willYouForgiveMeIf(
    "I give you space?");
abigail.willYouForgiveMeIf(
    "I pretend that nothing happened?");
```

If I had to guess
Abigail's `method` is a short one.
No matter what `argument` I give
it always returns `false`.

Anxious

I've lost the one person
who makes me feel like
I belong.

At dinner
I chew on a flower of broccoli
making it last all through the meal
by taking a bite
and then spending far too long
picking the green bits out of my teeth.

And tonight
I'm not the only one.

Dad looks at the two of us
me and Mom
with almost full plates
and asks {
   "Are you two okay?";
}

I nod
Mom nods
we nod.

Fine

Mom gets another call.

Dad smiles
shakes his head
takes a bite of his baked potato.

But I don't think it's funny.

I give Mom a look
so sharp
so out of tune
it's like my eyes are saying {
   "Are you really going to answer that?";
}
and Mom gives me a look back
her buttoned-up mouth
saying {
   "What choice do I have?";
}

She picks up her phone
*mm-hmm*s a few times from the other room
then hangs up.

She sits back down.
Cuts off a piece of her pork chop.
Pokes her fork into it.
Raises it to her mouth.

Then she stops
lowers her fork
and pulls out her computer.

```
String[] whatIHearFromMyBedroom =

{

    "Do they really expect you to work such long
     hours?",

    "I need to be on call whenever my boss
     needs me.",

    "Does that mean you can't sometimes say no?",

    "When I'm this new, that's exactly what it
     means.",

    "If you really feel like you need to, then
     of course you have my support.",

    "Thank you.",

    "I just hate that I'm making you do this.",

    "You're not making me do anything.",

    "I know, but you wouldn't have to do this if
     it weren't for me.",
```

"Let me worry about the money for a change. You just worry about the music.",

"That reminds me! I think I may have found another private lesson client today.",

"That's great!",

"So hopefully this job is only temporary.",

"Yeah, I hope so too."
};

Da Capo

When I wake up the next day
I feel new.
Fresh.

Like I'm the most
me
that I've been in ages.

I'm still upset
that Abigail's not speaking to me
but also I'm starting to feel like
maybe I didn't do anything wrong.

Or maybe I did do something wrong
but so did Abigail.

Or maybe Abigail isn't so much mad at me
as she is at herself.

Or maybe
this whole thing
isn't quite boolean.

And maybe
I can fix it.

Silver Lining

I think I'll go back
to sandwiches for my lunch.

I don't like weird grains.

Argument One

In homeroom
Abigail sits by herself.

I ask myself
What would I want
if I were Abigail?

```
abigail.willYouForgiveMeIf(
    "I sit by you in homeroom?");
```

False

Abigail raises her hand
asks if she can go to the nurse's office
because something in the room
is giving her a headache.

Not a Coincidence

Ms. Delaney's hands fly today
faster than normal
as if she can feel that things are off
with me and Abigail
and everything.

She's rubbing her temples
when we walk in
and the lights are dimmed
but she pretends they're not
as she asks {
    "Is there any such thing
     as 'random'?";
}
She flips a coin
which comes up heads
and asks {
    "Was it random?";
}

I nod yes
and so do Iain and Drake
and Francis and Evan
but I don't look at Abigail
because she is not sitting next to me today.

Random Numbers

Ms. Delaney says {
   "What does it mean if I told you
   that the Giants had a 10 percent chance
   of winning the World Series?

   If we were to clone this world ten times
   would the Giants win in exactly one of them?
   Or is a Giants' victory set in stone?
   Maybe they'd win in all ten!

   And what does it mean if there's a 90 percent chance
   that they win
   but they end up losing?
   Maybe they never had a shot in the first place
   and the 90 percent
   was just an illusion.

   Does "randomness" even exist?
}

We're quiet now
because even though Ms. Delaney is asking
questions
it doesn't seem like she wants
answers.

{
    "In computers
    true randomness
    doesn't exist.
    Random numbers are generated
    from an `algorithm`.
    It's good enough for practical purposes
    but it's not really *random*.

    So what does it mean
    for the randomness in our own lives
    if computers can't perfectly simulate it?
    How are we supposed to think about
    happenstance
    coincidence
    and plain old bad luck
    if we can't model it on a computer?";
}

Ms. Delaney opens her mouth
closes it.
I look to where Abigail usually sits
but she's not next to me today
and when Ms. Delaney finally convinces
her mouth to speak
I know before she says anything
that this was never really about computers.

Ms. Delaney Is Sick

and I feel sick too.

Pianissimo

When she was diagnosed
she quit her job
and when she got better
she never went back.

She didn't think it would come back.

It wasn't supposed to come back.

There was a 90 percent chance it wouldn't come back.

She was supposed to have years!
Ten
twenty
fifty years where she could forget.

And now that she can't
well
there's medication
and surgery
and there's new treatments coming out every year.

It wasn't supposed to come back
but somehow it has.

Wrong

I look over to Abigail
across the room.
But her eyes are pointed down
and Ms. Delaney wears a practiced smile
and it's like no matter where I look
everything feels `false`.

Argument Two

Abigail sits
alone
at a table in the corner
and I join her.

```
abigail.willYouForgiveMeIf(
    "I sit by you at lunch?");
```

False

Even though
I'm sure
she's just as upset
about Ms. Delaney
as I am

she still takes her lunchbox
and stomps away.

Things That Are False

```java
if ( Mom asks about how school was ) {
    System.out.println("Fine");
}
```

Requiem

All
weekend
long
I
reach
for
my
variables.
They
usually
make
me
happy
but
today
whenever
I
remember {
    Ms. Delaney;
    the computer lab;
    Abigail;
}
I
hit
void.

Breakfast, Lunch, and Dinner

```
stomach.settle();
```

A Bad Weekend

```
while ( It is still the weekend )  {
    if ( mom ) {
        mom.typeFromTheCouch();
        mom.mmHmmOnThePhone();
        mom.hideYourselfInTheOffice();
    }

    if ( dad ) {
        dad.playYourSong();
        dad.playYourSong();
        dad.playYourSong();
    }

    if ( emmy ) {
        emmy.program();
        emmy.tryToEat();
        emmy.worry();
    }
}
```

Griiiiiiiiiiiiiind: Remix

Dad's working on a tricky little part of his new song.
He's playing it on repeat
like if he can just get it perfectly
they'll call him in to perform.

I wish he'd play louder
because I can still hear Mom's phone ring.

I can still hear her car pull out of the garage.

I can still hear the sound
my computer makes when I get a notification
even though Abigail hasn't messaged me in days.

And worst of all
I can still hear Ms. Delaney
telling us she's sick.

Dad plays his tricky little part
over
and over
and over
stopping himself when he makes a mistake
which seems to happen earlier
and earlier

and earlier
earlier
and earlier
earlier
earlier
until

BANG!

he smashes his hands on the piano.

It's the first time Dad has made
our ugly yellow piano
actually sound ugly.

Halloween

When it was Halloween back home
I would dress up with my friends.

We would make pumpkin sugar cookies
out of jack-o'-lantern guts
(mua-ha-ha!)
and watch every horror movie on Netflix
rated PG-13 or below.

We would listen to Dad play
"The Monster Mash"
and he would harmonize with Mom
on the *aah-ooh*s.

Halloween used to be
something I looked forward to every year.

But today
I try to forget about it.
I don't have anyone to dress up with
and I'm not in the mood to make cookies
or watch Netflix.
Plus
all Dad wants to play
is his new song.

I was doing a good job forgetting about Halloween
by spending the night doing math homework
until I heard a *thunk*
and a *splat*
and a *crack*
on our door.

Looks like someone egged our house.

Mua-ha-ha.

What Friends Are For

On Monday
Abigail doesn't even show up
to homeroom.

And if I know my friend
I know where she's hiding.

< 271 >

Knocks Me Off My Feet

I force myself to walk
one step at a time

    left, and right, and left, and right, and left

until I find a girl
in braids
hiding
under the stairs.

I open my mouth
to apologize
for the cafeteria
for breaking her cover
for telling her secret
but before I can
Abigail jumps
arms out
and wraps them around my neck
in a hug.

Emmy and Abigail: The Apology Duet

I'm sorry I
blew your cover.

It wasn't my secret to tell!

It wasn't fair of me.

I guess I felt
jealous.

You're such a good singer
and you have all these friends.

I wish I were cool
like you.

You think I'm confident?
I don't feel confident.
                But I do feel
sorry.

I'm sorry.
I'm sorry.
          I'm sorry.

I'm sorry I
made you keep my secret.

You never should have
had to keep it at all!

It wasn't fair of me.

I guess I felt
embarrassed.

You're such a good coder
and you're always yourself.

I wish I were confident
like you.

You think I'm cool?
Well, I don't feel cool.

sorry.

I'm sorry.
I'm sorry.

Emmy and Abigail: The Apology Coda

I'm also   I'm also

    worried   worried

         about   about

       Ms. Delaney.

When You're Sick

Sometimes
when you're sick
boys that are only in your class
because their mom is making them
realize just how much
they've needed their time in the computer lab
in spite of themselves.

And sometimes
those boys
show up for extra lessons {
    "Evan! Come on in!";
}

The New Schedule

```
if ( It's lunchtime ) {
    if ( It's Tuesday || Thursday ) {
        emmy.goToTheComputerLab();
        emmy.eatYourTurkeyAndCheeseSandwich();
        emmy.learnAboutComputers()
            && emmy.learnAboutEvan()
            && emmy.learnAboutDrake()
            && emmy.learnAboutIain()
            && emmy.learnAboutMsDelaney()
            && emmy.learnAboutAbigail()
            && emmy.learnAboutEmmy();
    } else if ( It's Monday || Wednesday || Friday ) {
        emmy.goToTheCafeteria();
        emmy.eatWithAbigail();
        emmy.lookAtAbigailsOldTable()
            && emmy.pretendYouAreNotWatchingThem();
    }
}
```

Separate Methods: Remix

Sometimes I wish
we could spend every lunch period
in the computer lab

        because I hate seeing Abigail's face

        when she watches her friends talk

        and laugh

        and sometimes sing

        over at her old table.

Sometimes I wish
I were three different people

        because then our table would be big

        and loud

        like all the other tables in the cafeteria

        and maybe Abigail wouldn't miss her old

        one as much.

Sometimes I wish
I were in Abigail's choir

        because I know she's been lonely there too

        without her old friends.

Sometimes I wish I had never revealed
her secret

        because I miss them being my friends too.

Not So Separate

Sometimes I wonder
if maybe things aren't
as good over there
as they'd like us to think
          because sometimes
          when I look over at them
          they're looking right back at us.

Above

On Thursday in homeroom
the giggling girls
the musical girls
the Option A girls
aren't giggling.
They aren't talking about music

or anything much at all.

Every time Rebecca starts to say something
Angel remembers
she needs something in her backpack
and then Divya becomes preoccupied
with the sheet music she's studying
and Rebecca goes silent again.

But Abigail and I
me and Abigail
don't spend much time thinking about them
because Abigail brought in Bob
our raspberry pi robot
to show to Ms. Delaney
and we take it out
before first period starts
because we can be each other's
Option A.

Subject: Doctor Appointment Today

To My Amazing Wonderful Brilliant Computer Scientists,

I'm so sorry I have to leave a little bit early and won't be able to make our club time today. Don't let the suddenness of this cancellation concern you. Everything is okay; my doctor just had a sudden cancellation of his own and we were able to move one of my appointments up.

But for some good news, the computer lab happens to be free after class tomorrow. So for those of you who are available, I'll see you then for our rescheduled computer club.

—Ms. Delaney

Full

We spend lunch at our usual table
but it's nice having a third person
    even if he is a robot
to keep us company.

We make him walk across the table
get right up close to the edge inch by inch until he

                  f
                a
                  l
                    l
                s
          into our hands
            waiting
           to catch him.

At our two-person
    well
    two-and-a-half-person
table
we laugh so hard
there's no room
for empty space.

New Friend

We're laughing so hard
playing with Bob
that we aren't wasting time
watching
the Option A group.

If we had been
maybe we would have seen it coming.

The slamming of a lunch tray
the screeching of a kicked chair
and the scream of {
   "TOO BAD!";
}

Rebecca walks
across a silent cafeteria
over to our table.

She sits down
across from Bob
and says {
   "Angel seems to think
    she's the boss of me.
    Well, she's not.

And I can't figure out
why the fact that I still want to audition
for the Honey Bees
in a month
should stop me from sitting with
you
my friends
and playing with
your robot
today.";
}

True

On Friday after class
before our rescheduled club time
Abigail leaves
and when she comes back
she's not alone.

She's with
Rebecca.

She asks {
    "Is it okay if my friend hangs out here today?";
}

And Ms. Delaney says {
    "The answer to that question
      is always yes.";
}

Rebecca

Rebecca jumps in
feet first
asking questions
every ten seconds
so Ms. Delaney will go off on tangents
that make her hands jump and burst
until we're so far away from where we started
that we don't even remember it {
    "Why do they call them `methods`?";

    "Why are some words purple
     and others black?";

    "What are those cards on your desk for?";
}

```
public =
```

Ms. Delaney is sick.
I guess it was never really a secret
but somehow it has become
```
public.
```

Like the first word of my song.

Public: A keyword denoting that a method or variable is
visible for general consumption.

Ms. Delaney's illness
is now visible for general consumption.
It belongs to everyone.
The cards on her desk are from teachers
and parents
and students
who don't even know her.

```
msDelaney.getWellSoon();
msDelaney.feelBetter();
msDelaney.miraclesCanHappen();
```

And as the days crawl on
and the pile of cards
gets bigger

and bigger

and bigger

I feel like I'm the one
that's going to be sick.

```
String[]
whatIHearWhenIPassThePrincipalsOffice=
```

{

"Are you sure you can keep working?",

"The doctors said I can keep working as long as I want to. And right now, I want to.",

"Look, we're happy to have you stay...",

"Perfect! I'm glad we agree.",

"But what about going forward? You've already missed a couple of classes and isn't it just going to get worse?",

"I have a visit with a specialist over Thanksgiving break. I'll know more after that.",

"Frankie, think of the students.",

"I only think of the students."

};

Building

Ms. Delaney tells us what our assignment will be
for the last month
of the semester {
    "You're going to make games.
    Ping-Pong or
    Brick or
    —yes, Abigail—
    Tetris.";
}

We will have a showcase
before winter break.
Date still to be decided.
We'll show off our games.

I have a question.
Abigail has a question.
We all have a question.
It's an obvious sort of question
but one that takes guts
or at least white sp—

Ms. Delaney has moved on
determined
to get us through the lesson.

Fluent

Ms. Delaney is explaining
how to move shapes around the screen
using `void methods`.
Commands like {

```
    circle.show();
    triangle.hide();
    rectangle.move(100, 150);
}
```

She shows us how to check for object collisions
using `methods` with return values.
Questions like {

```
    boolean collision = isColliding();
    boolean border = didHitBorder();
    int distance = getDistanceBetweenCenters(
        circle, square);
}
```

She shows us how to make our screens respond
to button presses
by filling in the `onClick` or `onKeyPress` `methods`.

But the crazy part
is that none of this feels hard.
None of this feels new.

None of this feels like a language

that I do not speak.

And when I say this

Ms. Delaney gives me one of those smiles

special for me

and says {

    "That's because you DO speak it, Emmy.

    You have the building blocks

    and now it's just about what you want to build.";

}

Final Bell

```
while ( The time > 11:15 a.m. && the time < 12:00 p.m. ) {
```
    Enjoy the time in the computer lab
    but feel the termination
    coming closer
    and closer.

    Thanksgiving break starts tomorrow
    and something tells me
    that it's more than just the `while` loop
    that's coming to a close.
```
}
```

So Close I Can Taste It

Thanksgiving break feels like
"In the Hall of the Mountain King."

It starts off slow
plodding
each day like a week.

Abigail's visiting cousins in Kansas City
Dad's practicing his song
Mom's at the office
and I'm bored.

Plod
      Plod
            Plod

But on Monday I start coding my game for Ms. Delaney
and before I know it
Monday is gone in the blink of an eye.
Tuesday and Wednesday are spent
building a physics engine
and Thursday is spent alternating between
debugging collision detection
and basting the turkey.

By Friday my game is nearly finished

and by Saturday

well

Saturday moves so fast

I can practically hear the cymbals crashing

the drum rolls vibrating

the violins tripping over themselves

to keep up with the conductor's waving arms

and as soon as the orchestra lands its final **chords**

on Sunday

my game is done

and I can't wait

to show Ms. Delaney

how far I've come.

Right

In homeroom it feels like
singing in **four-four time**
to a song I know by heart
in the key of C.

No sharps
no flats
everything like home.

I have conversations with kids
who know my name
about their breaks
and the homeroom teacher
Ms. Li
even asks me
by name
how my game is going
for computer science.

I sit with Abigail
and Rebecca
and even Divya
who had a fight with Angel over the break
about how Divya wants to help out with the play
after school two nights a week.

Sometimes they talk about the SFCC
and about the audition for the Honey Bees in a few weeks.
Rebecca is still going to audition for sure
Divya says she probably will
but it might depend on schedules for the play
and Abigail says she still doesn't know yet.

But what I know
is that for the first time
in so many days
things are starting to feel
right.

Wrong

When I walk into the classroom
I don't see Ms. Delaney.

Instead
I see Principal Fitzpatrick
and those thoughts
of showing Ms. Delaney
my finished game
evaporate.

It's like some happy piano string
just went

```
string.snap();
```

Fine

```
    String principalFitzpatricksSpeech =
```
"Everything is fine, children. Everything is fine. Don't you worry about your teacher, she's going to be fine, just you wait and see. Just a touch of fatigue, nothing to worry about. She didn't want to worry you, of course, so I'll stay right here and supervise while you work on your games. Yes, yes, don't look so surprised, I know you're working on games. See? Would Ms. Delaney have been able to tell me that if she wasn't feeling fine? I told you so, didn't I tell you? She'll be fine, now I'll just sit here in this chair and you all go on ahead and work. See? Nothing to worry about. Everything is going to be just fine.";

Frozen

I get home from school
and lie down on the couch.

I don't take off my shoes.
I don't turn on the TV.
I don't do anything at all.

I am void.

Not Fine

I guess I fall asleep
because when I wake up
I'm covered by a blanket.

Dad is playing "Clair de Lune"
and Mom is cooking dinner
home early
for the first time in a month.

She's doing hamburgers on the grill
because it's just that beautiful outside
even though it's the first week of December.

And when I walk past the door to the patio
Mom asks me how my day was.

I step outside
wrap my arms around her torso
and push my nose into the smell
of laundry detergent and perfume.

My mouth muffled
I say {
    "Awful.";
}

Substitute

I hate the word *substitute*.
There is no such thing.

He says {
    "Your teacher
    Ms. Delaney
    will
    almost certainly
    be back
    by the end of the week.
    And in the meantime
    I assure you
    I am more than qualified
    to help you finish your games.";
}

But the way he says *games*
makes them sound small
and not like something
we've been working toward for months.

And the way he says *finish*
makes it sound as though
he's not just here for the day.

Oh, By the Way . . .

. . . he adds {
   "Ms. Delaney booked the cafeteria
   during lunch on Friday, December 17
   for your showcase.
   A little over two weeks from today.

   From what Ms. Delaney tells me
   it's going to be exciting!
   You get to present your games to each other
   and your families if they can come
   plus because it's during lunchtime
   you'll be able to show them off
   to the whole school!";
}

Abigail whispers to me {
   "That's the same time as the Honey Bee auditions.";
} but I can barely hear her
because I'm still stuck on the part
where we are presenting our games
to
the
whole
school.

Emmy's Fairy Tale

Once upon a time there were two young musicians who could play music so beautiful they could make a statue smile.

One day, they had a daughter, who grew up to believe she was a musician too. After all, she was their daughter, and she loved music more than anything else in the whole world. But whenever she would try to make music, people would stuff their fingers into their ears and call her a waste of such musical blood.

But the girl kept making music because she loved it, and she knew that if she just kept working at it, eventually it would love her back. Until one day, while the girl was on stage, in the middle of her first-ever solo, her head began to fuzz, her vision began to spot, her tongue began to tingle then   trip

       and

         she

           fainted.

When she woke up, she swore she would never, ever, *ever* step foot on stage again. And she didn't need to! She discovered a music all her own that she could play from a different sort of keyboard.

And as far as she knew, she would live happily ever after.

THE END

```
String whatEmmySaysToAbigail =
```

"I absolutely positively one hundred percent
cannot step foot on stage at the showcase.";

Absent

When I'm coding
I forget about my stage fright.

I don't picture the audience
cocking their heads
squinting their eyes
twisting their mouths.

I don't picture anything
except the code.

So even though my game is done
I find more work to do.
I build in a two-player mode
and a way to compete
against the computer.
I add colors
difficulty levels
and sound effects
because the more I code
the less I think about how
I can't go on stage.

I absolutely can't.

And even if I could

there's no point

because everyone

I would want to show my game to {

    Abigail,

    Mom,

    Dad,

    Ms. Delaney

} may not even be there

at all.

The Worst Schedule

```
if ( It's Monday || Wednesday || Friday before lunch )  {
    emmy.programPingPong();
    emmy.programPingPong();
    emmy.programPingPong();
} else {
    emmy.worry();
}
```

90 Percent

The substitute
whose name does not matter
says there is a 90 percent chance
Ms. Delaney will be back in class next Monday.
And in any case
she left the next week's lesson plan
in a massive three-ring binder
so we won't have to pause our work
on the off-chance
that she takes a little longer
to recover.

But if Ms. Delaney taught us anything
it's that 90 percent
means nothing.

10 percent

If there is a 90 percent chance of something
and it doesn't happen
does that mean
that things just
somehow
went against the plan?
Or is there someone
pulling the strings
laughing himself sick
over our
rotten
luck?

Emails: Opus 2

My inbox is full
of emails from teachers
alerting us
that even though our final projects
aren't due until
finals
that doesn't mean that we shouldn't start working on them
yesterday.

My inbox is full
of pictures
of shouting students
wearing yellow and brown
at our latest soccer game
—Go Bumblebees!—
from the daily *Hive Mind*.

My inbox
has three unread emails
(3)
from Ms. Delaney.

Subject: The Next Week

My Amazing and Brilliant Computer Scientists,

I hope you're all working hard on your projects!

I'm sure you're all wondering how I'm doing, and the answer is that I'm doing better and better every day. This week we are trying out a new medication, and I'm at home now, resting, just until we decide that it's working. If things go as well as we hope they will, I'll be back next week, well before the showcase. In the meantime, I'm sending Mr. Hobart, your substitute, daily emails detailing any questions that might pop up, so keep working hard and make me proud!

Computationally yours,
Ms. Delaney

Subject: Pi

My Extraordinary and Virtuosic Computer Scientists,

I was killing time today and so I decided to figure out how to generate the first 1,000 digits of pi in a dozen different computer languages. For your amusement, I've attached my Java code below and here are the first 500 digits of pi:

```
3141592653589793238462643383279502884197169399375105820974944592307816406286208998628034825342117067982148086513282306647093844609550582231725359408128481117450284102701938521105559644622948954930381964428810975665933446128475648233786783165271201909145648566923460348610454326648213393607260249141273724587006606315588174881520920962829254091715364367892590360011330530548820466521384146951941511609433057270365759591953092186117381932611793105118548074462379962749567351885752724891227938183011949129834
```

Infinitely yours,

Ms. Delaney

```java
private static final int SCALE = 10000;
private static final int ARR_INIT_VAL = 2000;
public static String piDigits(int digits) {
    StringBuffer piBuffer = new StringBuffer();
    int[] digitArray = new int[digits + 1];
    int carry = 0;
    for (int i = 0; i <= digits; ++i) {
        digitArray[i] = ARR_INIT_VAL;
    }
    for (int i = digits; i > 0; i -= 14) {
        int sum = 0;
        for (int j = i; j > 0; --j) {
            sum = sum * j + SCALE * digitArray[j];
            digitArray[j] = sum % (j * 2 - 1);
            sum /= j * 2 - 1;
        }
        piBuffer.append(
            String.format("%04d", carry + sum / SCALE));
        carry = sum % SCALE;
    }
    return piBuffer.toString();
}
public static void main(String[] args) {
    int n = args.length > 0
        ? Integer.parseInt(args[0]) : 100;
    System.out.println(piDigits(n));
}
```

Subject: One More Thing

My Dazzling and Luminous Computer Scientists

It's never too early to start thinking about how you want to change the world! So if any of you want to tackle fixing the ridiculous software that my doctors are using to try to track my medication, you have my blessing!

Technologically yours,
Ms. Delaney

Infinite Loop

```
if ( emmy.isWorriedAboutMsDelaney() ) {
    emmy.spendMoreTimeOnPingPong();
}
```

The Main Method

In the cafeteria
the methods have dispersed.

```
public static void main(String[] args) {
    emmy.sitWithIain();
    emmy.sitWithDivya();
    emmy.sitWithEvan();
    emmy.sitWithRebecca();
    emmy.sitWithDrake();
    emmy.sitWithAbigail();

    emmy.evenSitWithFrancis();

    everyone.programYourGames();
    everyone.together();
}
```

A Method Apart

On Wednesday during lunch
Abigail walks up to
Angel
who is sitting by herself
fingers in her ears
humming
the soprano part
to the Honey Bee audition piece
"The Little Birch Tree."

Abigail says {
    "How's your part coming?";

    "I'm still not sure if I'm going to audition.";

    "Do you want to come sit with us?
     Maybe we could practice together?";

    "I guess that's a no.
     Let me know if you change your mind.
     You're always welcome.";
}

Games

After weeks of working together
in the cafeteria
during lunch
I'm not the only one
whose game is finished.

Abigail has finished her game too
&& Evan
&& Iain
&& Drake
&& Francis
&& even Rebecca && Divya.

Our games are done
but no one can be happy about it
because that means the showcase is just around the corner
and the only one here to see our games

is no substitute.

Rest

When the bell rings
we stay at the table
for an extra breath.

Drake says {
    "We need to show them to her.";
}

Evan says {
    "She said she'll be back in time for the showcase.";

    "She wouldn't miss the showcase for anything.";
}

Abigail says {
    "But just in case?";
}

Evan says {
    "I'll think of a way.";
}

Two-Part Dissonance

Dad is practicing
his tricky little part
over and over and over.
He plays it slow
and then faster and faster and faster until
he messes up
and plays it
slow
again.

He's just about got it
all the way through
when the phone rings.

The music

freezes
and it takes him just
a breath too long
to answer the phone {
    "It's okay.
    Take your time.
    I love you too.";
}

The Note

On Thursday morning
I open up my locker
and out falls a stack of paper cards
cut to look like plane tickets
filled with punched-out holes.

I know it's a note from Abigail
so I don't ask her for help
and instead
I spend all my free time
in the library

researching.

ecret-Say ode-Cay

Punch cards are easy to read
once you get the hang of it.

Each line is a letter
spelled out in binary.

Hole=1; Gap=0;

And if you count the letters in the alphabet

A=1   B=2   C=3   . . . .   Z=26

and convert those counts to binary

A=1   B=01   C=11   . . . .   Z=11010

and make them all one byte
which means make them all eight bits
which means make them all eight digits

A=00000001 B=00000010 C=00000011   . . .   Z=00011010

add in the binary value for the space character 00100000

and before you know it

```
00001101 00000101 00000101
00010100 00100000 00001001
00001110 00100000 00001100
00001111 00000010 00000010
00011001 00100000 00000001
00010100 00100000 00010100
00001000 00010010 00000101
         00000101
```

becomes

. . .

. . .

. . .

Decoded

```
M       E       E
T       B       I
N       R       L
O       E       B
Y               A
T               T
H               E
```

Lipsticks

I was expecting Abigail
standing with her arms crossed
at the front of the pack
leading us in her grand plan.

But when I see her standing
with Divya && Rebecca && Iain && Francis
each holding their punch card note
she looks just as confused as I do.
She asks {
    "Do you know what's going on?
     We have choir practice tonight.
      Angel's mom will be here any minute.";
} and I say no
because I don't.

Until
I hear
a voice {
    "Ready to go visit Ms. Delaney?";
}

Evan stands next to Drake
laptop in one hand
a CVS bag in another.

Their fingers are covered in blisters
and graphite
probably from poking holes in all those papers
but they are smiling
wider than I've ever seen them before.

Or maybe it just looks that way
because their cheeks are decorated
in candy-apple-red lipstick.

Exclusive Or

Maybe when a waiter asks
soup or salad
you can just say
"Yes!"
but sometimes *or*
just means one.

Abigail looks at Divya
who looks at Rebecca
who looks back at Abigail
who says {
    "I think this is more important
      than choir practice.";
}

Forgiveness: Remix

We smear our faces
in candy-apple red
decorating each other's cheeks with hearts
stars
and treble clefs.

When we're done
everyone's face is the color of **fortissimo.**

Everyone
that is
except
Francis.

Evan gives him a hard time
telling him that everyone else is doing it
and that we're supposed to look silly
that's kind of the point
but the way that Francis avoids eye contact
with me
makes me think
that maybe forgiving someone else
is a lot more boolean
than forgiving yourself.

```
String whatISayToFrancis =
```

"That's okay, Francis. You can wait until
you're ready.";

Come In

We get to Ms. Delaney's house
and press the buzzer.

bzzzzzzzzzzzzzzzzzzzzzzzz

The parents wait in the lobby
next to the hand-crank elevator
while we take the stairs
        up
   up
up
until we see a door open
just a crack
but we pause.

```
while ( No one has knocked yet ) {
    everyone.straightenYourBacks();
    everyone.unclenchYourHands();
    everyone.pretendToKnowWhatToExpectInside();
}
```

Evan knocks
and a voice comes from the crack.
One we recognize

and yet don't {
    "Come in.";
}

We push the door open
sl-
    -o-
            -o-
                -o-
                    -w
to see what happens
now that our `while` loop has
terminated.

Tonal Music

Ms. Delaney's condo is small
brightly lit
made with wood and glass
and every inch
of every wall
is covered
in art.

Multicolored
chaotic
and while each picture is different
when they are all together
they complement each other.
They harmonize.

I look at Drake
who is noticing it too
and points to one in particular that looks familiar.

It's up high
and slightly crooked
and maybe it's just because I recognize it
glowing faintly purple on the wall
but I swear
it's the most beautiful picture I've ever seen.

Forgetting

We haven't even seen Ms. Delaney yet
but from behind me
I hear Francis say {
   "I forgot something in the car.
    Meet you in there in a minute.";
}

A Wrong Note

I don't mean to do it
but when I see Ms. Delaney
come out from the kitchen
I make the ugly piano face.

My head cocks
my eyes squint
my mouth twists.

I don't like
that Ms. Delaney's clothes hang on her like a tent
that her cheekbones are sharp and pointed

that Ms. Delaney
isn't wearing
her lipstick.

Allegro

But just then
Francis comes back in the house
his face covered
so fully
in candy-apple red
that it fills the whole room.

And when Ms. Delaney says {
   "It's so good to see you!";
} she smiles
so big
so **bold**
it paints a cherry streak in the air anyway.

{
   "It's so good
   to see
   my Computers in Lipstick.";
}

A Closer Look

We demo our games
in five-minute intervals
because Ms. Delaney warned us
the medicine makes her sleepy
and she doesn't know how long she can last.

For each one
she plays it through
oohs and aahs
in a way that the substitute never does {

    "Wouldn't it be cool if . . .";

    "You should try . . .";

    "If you want an extra challenge . . .";
}

I go last
because everyone else wants to go first
and also because all I can think of
is that *this* is the showcase I care about
the one with the person
the people
who for the first time ever
make me feel like I belong.

Fun Facts: Remix

I show my game.
Ms. Delaney oohs and aahs
but I can't focus
because the air feels quiet.

My game gently pings
and pongs
but there's something stuck
like a song in my head.

So this time
instead of muffling it
I let it out {
(#1)
    "This time last year
        I was still in Wisconsin
        and I wasn't sure
        if I would fit in here.
        If I'd find friends
        or be happy at all.
        But
(#2)
    I'm happier now
        than I've ever been.
        So I guess you're right

Ms. Delaney
that sometimes life has
mixed-up ways
of telling you where you're *not* supposed to be.
And maybe it's not fair
for me to say three fun facts
when everyone else only got one
but I'd be remiss if I didn't mention that
(#3)
I have a dog named Jeopardy
and one time my mom filmed us dancing in the kitchen
and the YouTube video
just hit fifty thousand views.";

}

No Telling

Ms. Delaney's eyes are drooping
but even so
she smiles

HUGE

until the parents give us
our final warning.

We say our *see you later*s
our *ta-ta for now*s.
I squeeze her hand and say {
    "Hello, Ms. Delaney!";
} and as we're out the door Evan adds in {
    "Imagine how much better the games will be
      when you're back for the showcase next week!";
}

Ms. Delaney nods
but I can tell from the way
her teeth button her lips
that there's no telling when
she's coming back.

Subito Piano

Tonight
when I get home
Dad gets the phone call he's been waiting for.

It's his big break.

He's on at eight.

The Grind

There is a moment
of joy.

Our soundtrack is **allegro**
andante
presto
vivace.

I smile so hard my cheeks hurt
and Mom laughs so hard
she cries.

It would have been perfect
if Mom's phone
hadn't rung
ten seconds later.

Attempted Duet No. 7

"Dad, should I get ready to—"

        "Emmy, why don't you go to your room."

Arguments: Remix

```
public
static
void
main
String
bracket
bracket...

args.
```

An argument is a fight.

An argument is what comes between two married people.

An argument is what Mom and Dad are in right now.

What I Hear from My Bedroom

"This performance is a big deal to me."

        "I know, and I'm not going to miss
        it I swear!"

"This is the whole reason we moved here!"

        "I know, and I'll be there
        as soon as I can!"

"I don't understand why your boss
can't take care of himself just this once."

        "Because it's my job to help him.
        Trust me, if I thought I could say no
        I would have done it already."

"I don't know what I was expecting.
I mean, we knew this job would be time-consuming
but you're doing it all for me."

        "I didn't do it *all* for you."

"No, you should be singing
not working for some jerk
who thinks your time belongs to him.
And you wouldn't have to
if I hadn't brought us here.
Or if I could have found a job
that guaranteed stage time!"

        "But that doesn't mean I'm doing
        this for you."

"What do you mean?"

"I'm doing this for us."

Fortissimo

I put on my headphones
and turn my music up so loud
I can't hear myself think.

I can't hear myself wonder
what does it mean for me
when even Mom is having trouble
figuring out where she belongs.

Attempted Trio

"What's going on?"

> "Just get ready to go."

"Shouldn't we wait for Mom?"

> "Please just get ready."

"She's not going to miss it, is she?
She wouldn't.
She can't."

> "Emmy.
> Please.
> We need to go."

Lento: Remix

I grab my coat
and put on my shoes
sl-
    -o-
        -o-
            -o-
                -w
and when we're almost out the door
I give Mom a look
that couldn't be further from **allegro**.

She looks back at me
with apology eyes
and says {
    "I'll be there.
      I promise.";
}

Solo: Remix

I sit in the theater
front row
an empty seat next to me.

Two-Part Harmony: Remix

The lights go down
the curtain rises
and in a rush of scarves
and gloves
and a roar of applause
Mom collapses in her seat. {
    "Told you I'd be here.
    I wouldn't miss this
    for the world.";
}

The Symphony: Remix

The symphony
is the swishing and whirling of the harp's glissando
like swivel chairs on soft-carpet floors.
It's the tick-a-tick of the wood block
over the clickety-clack of six castanets.
It's the whispers of
the English horn   the violin   the oboe
so different
and yet somehow together
mixing and melding in three-quarter time.

And through it all
my heart beats along
boom-bah-dah
boom-bah-dah
boom
like it's the bass line
pounding
reminding me of the places
and the people
that make me feel like

I be-long
I be-long
I be-long.

4:33 a.m.

The show ended hours ago
and my eyes are drooping.
I have to be up soon to go to school
but I can't sleep
because the music inside of me is

surging

       m   g
     u   p   n
j   i

cha-
    cha-
        chaing

and I can't help thinking
about the silence in Ms. Delaney's house
as she was playing my game.
The sound effects are nice
the pings and pongs it makes
when the ball hits the wall
but why should my final project
be so quiet

when the music inside of me
is so loud?

So
while the rest of the house
is asleep
I pull out my computer.
With just a few notes played
on the keyboard
my game
makes music
and I spend the rest of the night
tapping my toe
to the rhythm of
my `algorithm`.

Emails: Opus 3

My inbox is full
of reminders
newsletters
announcements
homework.

But all next week
I check it every minute
until

(1)

Subject: The Showcase

Dear Computers in Lipstick,

I have some great news and some not-so-great news.

First, the great news: We have decided that it is finally time to pursue surgery. This is great news because I lucked into an appointment with the top surgeon in the entire world for this particular procedure. And once the surgery is done, we will know one way or another what my prognosis is, and knowledge is the best news in the world.

Now, the not-so-great news: The surgery is scheduled for the morning of the showcase.

Words cannot express how sorry I am to be missing your big day, as it has been the light at the end of a murky tunnel for me. But keep your eyes open after the showcase, because I'll email you all just as soon as I wake up, happy and healthy.

And, finally, I would be remiss if I didn't tell you that the mental image of you presenting your final projects makes me look toward the future with all the joy in the world.

Optimistically yours,
Ms. Delaney

(1): Remix

I check my email constantly.
I know there won't be news.
I know she hasn't yet left for New York
I know she hasn't yet gotten to the hospital
and as the days go on   and on   and on
my stomach twists   turns   and grinds.

But I keep the tab open
on my laptop
because I know how much rests on this surgery
I know what "prognosis" means
I know all this
and so
whenever my email flicks to
(1)
I check.

Reminders.
Newsletters.
Announcements.
Homework.

No news
is no news.

More Boolean Than Not

Things that are true {
    there will be a showcase;
    we will order pizza
        which I will eat
        no matter how terrified I am
        of stepping foot on stage;
    we will take over the cafeteria during lunch;
    our parents will spend
        their Friday lunch hours
        playing our games;
}

        Things that are false {
            when Evan asks
                if there's any way
                for Ms. Delaney
                to see our showcase
                all the way in New York City
                the substitute says {
                    "We'll see.";
                }
            }

Perfect Pitch

It's after dinner
and the showcase is in two days.
I should be writing an essay
I have due in English class
or studying for an algebra test next week
or at the very least I should be going to bed
so I'll be well rested
when I faint on stage.
But instead of being productive
I'm tweaking the music I made for my game.

I don't hear her come in
but I hear her say {
    "What song is that?";
}

I swivel my chair
to see Mom
conducting with her eyes closed
in the lamplight {
    "It's nothing
        just something I've been playing with.";
}

Mom cocks her head
squints her eyes
twists her mouth {
   "Emmy
   is
   that
   yours?";
}

I nod
and move to stop
my game's background music
but Mom says {
   "Don't.
   Keep playing.
   It's beautiful.";
}

Booleans

The night before the showcase
Abigail calls in sick to choir rehearsal
and invites me over.
Just me
since the others didn't play hooky
but it's nice being just the two of us.

We play with Bob
tweak some of his code so he turns
so it looks like he's dancing
the twist.
When I ask Abigail
if she's made a decision yet
about whether to go to the showcase
or audition for the Honey Bees
she says {
   "Rebecca's auditioning.
    Divya is doing the play instead.
    And obviously Angel will be there.";
} as if that answers my question . . .
and I can almost feel
how strong her wish is
for things to be
boolean.

Binary

I wish everything were as simple
as my Ping-Pong game.
It's the most complicated thing
I've ever made
and yet it still boils down
to ones and zeroes.

Fitting In: Remix

We're supposed to dress up for the showcase.
Look professional.
So on the day of
I push through my closet
to find a dress that fits.
But none of them do.

Mom says {
    "Well, you've grown four inches in the last four months
     so I'm hardly surprised.";
}

And she's right.
I've changed this semester
in ways that I didn't even expect.
I pass Mom's shoulder now
instead of hitting just below.

And somehow
when I put on one of her old dresses
a candy-apple-red one
that swirls around my ankles
and swishes the carpet

I fit.

Infinite Loop: Remix

Mom's taking the day off
to come to the showcase.
She says {
   "I'm sick of being half here
   and half there.
   I'm taking today to be one hundred percent
   Mom.";
} but there is a moment
while Dad's driving us
to the school
that her phone rings.

She looks at it
touches it
looks at me

and lets it ring
and ring

               and ring

                            and ring.

Separate

Everything feels odd today
a half step flat
even though in every aspect other than the showcase
it's just an average Friday.

But it's not an average Friday.
Ms. Delaney's surgery should be over.
Any minute now
she could be waking up
she could be emailing us
telling us that she's happy
and healthy
and yet here I am
at school.

I know I'm different now
I know
I know
there are places where I belong
and even though I have to go on stage
in a matter of minutes
that's not the only thing I'm worried about.

< 364 >

What happens
if the surgery doesn't go
the way we hope?

If Ms. Delaney makes this city feel like home . . .

What if
            What if
                        What if?
So I sit down
just for a moment
just for a song
under my staircase.

Lift Me Up

{
    "What the heck do you think you're doing?";
}
I look up and see a girl.
A hand-out
    fingers-taut
        "Come with me" sort of girl.
A girl who today
made the decision
to listen to what she loves.

Abigail.

She's dressed up for the showcase
skirt skimming the floor
twelve new braids straight down her back
and bright purple stars
drawn on her cheeks.

I murmur something
about how I needed a minute
and Abigail says
with her alto-sax laugh {
    "If you think that I ditched Honey Bee auditions
     and maybe even lost

one of my oldest friends in the process
to let you spend a second of the showcase
under the stairs
by yourself
then you're nuts.

You belong in the cafeteria
with everyone else.";
}
With her right hand she lifts me up
and with her left she hands me
her bright purple lipstick.
{
    "Friends don't keep friends
    from the things they love.";
}

I take the lipstick out of her hand
smear the color on my cheeks
and say {
    "Race you!";
}

Programs

```java
public static void main(String[] args) {
    computersInLipstick.program();
}
```

Static

I'm showing my parents my code
at the lunch table where I once sat
by myself.
Hundreds and hundreds of lines
and I understand everything.

Well . . . almost everything.

static.

I was promised that one day
I would understand
every
single
word
of my song.
And now
static
is the only one left.

Nothing is static.
Everything is a variable.
Everything is always changing
moving around

and like a random number generator
it never gives you the same answer twice.

And even though `static`
turns purple on my screen
as I explain my code to my parents
it doesn't smile and nod to me
the way the other words do
because Ms. Delaney didn't have a chance
to teach us what it means.
And now I don't know
if Ms. Delaney will be back.

I don't know
if I'll ever learn.

We

We
(me and Abigail)
laugh.
We
(me and Francis)
talk.
We
(me and Drake)
smile.
We
(me and Dad and Mom)
tell jokes
share stories
play my game.
We
(the Computers in Lipstick)
know how much is riding on this surgery
and we
(the Computers in Lipstick)
check our email constantly
waiting for news
because we
(the Computers in Lipstick)
miss Ms. Delaney.

< 371 >

The Final Number

It's my turn
to go on stage.

To show my project.
To play my game.
To perform my music.

I walk up on stage
  left, and right, and left, and right, and left
and set up my computer
but my throat feels dry
and my hands feel shaky.

Abigail gives me a thumbs-up
in the sea of faces.
My parents wave
and it feels good to see
Iain
and Evan
and Drake
and even Francis
and the substitute teacher.

I imagine Rebecca singing her heart out
in the Honey Bee audition

and Divya painting a set piece
in a brilliant candy-apple red.
I even pretend I can hear Angel
acing her own audition
because why wouldn't she
when she's doing what she loves?

But for some reason
I can't make my mouth move.

There is so much white space.

There is too much white space.

fuzzy

                                       fuzzy

            and

                                            I

                       don't

            fast

                                      all

left

            will

                     be

fuzzy

if

do

something

that's

white space

So I hit the play button
on my game
filling the white space
with the music I created.

And before I have a chance
to stop myself
I sing along.

PUB-lic

STAT-ic

void, main, string.

BRACK-et

BRACK-et

ARGS

It's just my voice
a solo
but it's strong.
My head isn't fuzzy
my vision isn't spotty
and my music makes the room so full
that I can almost feel the floor rattle.

PUB-lic
STAT-ic
void, main, string.
BRACK-et
BRACK-et
ARGS

Before I know it
I'm not singing a solo anymore
because the Computers in Lipstick have joined me.
We are a choir
an orchestra
a symphony
and everyone else
looks at each other
confused.

PUB-lic
STAT-ic
void, main, string.
BRACK-et
BRACK-et
ARGS

I jump off the stage
take Abigail's hand in my right
Evan's in my left.
We hold on to each other
while the music **crescendoes**.

PUB-lic

STAT-ic

void, main, string.

BRACK-et

BRACK-et

ARGS

We sing
chant
program
in our main `method`
together

PUB-lic
STAT-ic
void, main, string.
BRACK-et
BRACK-et
ARGS

the music we learned
from Ms. Delaney.

PUB-lic

STAT-ic

void, main, string.

BRACK-et

BRACK-et

ARGS

While she conducts
from afar
we stand
hands interlocked
paused
static.

And when the music stops
and our voices fade
we're left holding each other
like a **fermata**
over the last note
in the world's
most beautiful
symphony.

Good News

I don't know what will happen next.
No one does.
But once our voices quiet
and the music beats on only in my chest
my smile is so **fortissimo**
I swear that everyone can hear it.

Boom-bah-dah
Boom-bah-dah
Boom.

And when the email tab
on my computer
still on the stage
flicks to
(1)
I breathe deep
because I know how lucky I am
to have found this place
these people
this moment
where I belong.

Author's Note

Thank you so much for reading *Emmy in the Key of Code*! This book is close to my heart because it combines the three subjects that I love most: code, music, and poetry.

When I was in school, we learned about these subjects in isolation. We had one class where we played music, a different class where we practiced writing, and a third class where we learned how to communicate with computers. And while I am so grateful that my school offered courses in subjects that turned out to be so important to me, I feel like this system of learning made it seem like these subjects were separate from one another, when in reality they are deeply intertwined.

Furthermore, we decide early in our lives that we are "good" at one subject and "bad" at another. I myself was "good" at math, and for years suppressed my budding love for writing. But in reality, if we love something, be it music, biology, basketball, or polka dancing, we may find that thing we love appearing in unexpected places. But only if we keep our eyes open.

So if there was something in this book that you found yourself drawn to, whether it was something you loved before you read Emmy's story or something you are just now considering, I hope with all my heart that you explore that interest.

If you keep reading, you'll find a glossary of computer and music terms that I used in this book. If you found a word that you didn't recognize, I hope you'll look it up! It may reveal a deeper layer to a poem that you missed on the first read.

And if you are interested in learning even more, here are some resources that can help guide your learning.

If you're interested in learning to program, ask your teachers if your school offers coding classes. If they do, take the course! If they don't, that's fine too, because there are plenty of resources available to anyone who wants to learn to program. For free online courses, check out Khan Academy, Code.org, Coursera, and MIT OpenCourseWare. If you're looking for an after-school class, check out theCoderSchool, Girls Who Code, Black Girls Code, Bootstrap, and Sylvan Learning Center. Or check with your local library to see if they have courses there.

If you're interested in learning how to play music, find out if your school offers music lessons. If they don't, you can learn by taking music lessons with a private teacher, singing with a church choir, or studying from online resources. Check out Coursera, Earmaster, and LightNote. There are also some great phone apps that can teach you the basics: Riffstation, Simply Piano, Vanido, and Tenuto. You can also find free music lessons on YouTube, and never underestimate the power of singing along with the radio.

And for further reading on the subject of the original Computers in Lipstick (or rather, the early women who made computer science what it is today), check out *Hidden Figures: The American Dream and the Untold Story of the Black Women Mathematicians Who Helped Win the Space Race* by Margot Lee Shetterly, *Ada Lovelace, Poet of Science: The First Computer Programmer* by Diane Stanley, and *Grace Hopper: Queen of Computer Code* by Laurie Wallmark.

Thank you again for reading my book. I hope it will help you to tell your own story, no matter if your language of choice is poetry, music, or Java.

Love,
Aimee

Glossary of Coding Terms

Algorithm: A series of instructions meant to solve a specific problem. Algorithms can be simple or complex. A simple one may be the algorithm to find the hypotenuse of a right triangle based off the length of its other two sides. A more complex one may be the algorithm used to find the shortest driving route from your house to school.

And (&&): And (&&) is used in `boolean` expressions, often in `if` statements or `while` loops, and the expression only evaluates to `true` if both conditions are `true`.

A simple example would be if you create two `boolean`s, a and b, and over the course of the program the values change. Then, later on, you want to see if they're both still `true`. You would do something like this:

```
boolean a = true;
boolean b = true;
    . . .
    . . .
    . . .
if (a && b) {
    System.out.println("Both are true!");
} else {
    System.out.println("At least one is false!");
}
```

Another, more complicated example would be if you want to print out all the numbers less than 100 that are divisible by 6. A number is divisible by 6 if it is divisible by both 2 and 3. So our code would look like this:

```
int i = 0;
while (i < 100) {
    if (i % 2 == 0 && i % 3 == 0) {
        System.out.println(i + " is divisible by 6");
    } else {
        System.out.println(i + " is not divisible by 6");
    }
}
```

(Args): The traditional name for the arguments passed into the main method. Fun fact: You don't have to call it `args`. You can call it whatever you want, as long as when you're referencing it in the code you always refer to the arguments by that same name.

Argument: Also called a "parameter," an argument is a variable passed into a method that can only be used inside that method. For example, the method `System.out.println("Emmy")` takes in one argument, a `String`, to be printed by the method.

Array: An array is a list of elements of a specific type. For example,

```
String[] names = new String[3];
```

creates a new array of ten strings. You can then set items in the array and store them for later use:

```
names[0] = "Emmy";
names[1] = "Abigail";
names[2] = "Ms. Delaney";
```

Then, later, when you want to read the items from the array, you can do that by indexing into the array. For example,

```
System.out.println(names[0]);
```

will print out **Emmy**.

Boolean: The smallest primitive type. It can only represent the values `true` or `false`.

Bracket Bracket: Represented by [] in Java, this symbol after a data type will let the computer know you want it to be an array—or in other words, a list—of that type. For example, if I want to create a variable to hold single `String`, I would do it like this:

```
String name = "Emmy";
```

But if I wanted to create a list of Strings, I would do it with the [] symbol.

```
String[] names = {"Emmy", "Abigail", "Ms. Delaney"};
```

Byte: A primitive type that holds less information than a `short`, but more information than a `boolean`. It can only represent integer values between –128 and 127.

Char: A primitive type in Java that is short for "character." A `char` in Java can be any letter or symbol on the keyboard, and even some that aren't on the keyboard, as long as they can be encoded using a system called UTF.

Curly Braces: The symbols { } that separate one chunk of code from another. For example,

```
public static void main(String[] args) {
    int i = 0;
    while (i < 10) {
        System.out.println(i);
        i = i + 1;
    }

}
```

Double: A primitive type like a float, but it contains double the amount of information.

Float: A primitive type that allows for decimal values and not just integers.

For: A for loop is a thin layer of code on top of a while loop. It behaves the same way, except a for loop contains three different expressions in its parenthetical. The first is the starting value of a variable, the second is the stopping condition, and the third is what to do to increment the value after each execution of the inner code. For example,

```java
void printNumbersOneThroughTen() {
    int[] numbers = {1, 2, 3, 4, 5, 6, 7, 8, 9, 10};
    for (int i = 0; i < numbers.length; i++) {
        System.out.println("number: " + numbers[i]);
    }
}
```

Global Variables: A type of variable that is declared at the top of your program and then can be used throughout the code. For example,

```java
String name = "Emmy";
public void printName() {
    System.out.println(name);
}

public void printNameWithAbigail() {
    System.out.println(name + " Abigail");
}
```

If you call `printName()` it would print **Emmy** and if you call `printNameWithAbigail()` it would print **Emmy Abigail** even though neither method declares the variable within itself.

Hello, World!: The first program that an engineer often wants to write in a new language is a simple program that will just output text. It has become tradition in the coding world for that text to be the phrase "Hello, World!" The first program I ever wrote was a Java program that said these words to me, and so I made it Emmy's first program as well.

IDE: An abbreviation for "integrated development environment." It's a term for the window in which a programmer will write their code. Think of it as Microsoft Word for computer programmers.

If: A statement in Java that evaluates an expression and performs one set of instructions if the expression evaluates to `true` and another set of instructions if the expression evaluates to `false`. For example,

```
int i = 0;
while (i < 10) {
    if (i % 2 == 0) {
        System.out.println(i + " is even");
    } else {
        System.out.println(i + " is odd");
    }
}
```

Infinite loop: If a snippet of code never terminates, it is said to be in an infinite loop. For example,

```
int i = 0;
while (true) {
    System.out.println(i);
    i = i + 1;
}
```

This bit of code will print out the integers, starting from 0, and never stop.

Int: A primitive type in Java that is short for "integer." An `int` in Java can be any integer (positive or negative) that is between the values -2^{31} and 2^{31-1}.

Long: A primitive type like an `int` except it contains double the amount of information. So it can represent numbers between -2^{63} and 2^{63-1}.

Main: The entry point of your program. It is the method that the computer calls when you tell the computer to run your program.

Method: A method is something that is callable on an object. For small programs, all your code can sit in the main method, but as your programs get bigger, that gets confusing and hard to read. Plus, if you want to do the same thing more than once, writing a method allows you to reuse code. And as your programs get really big, methods allow you to do all kinds of things, many of which are way beyond the scope of this book. But all methods are defined in the same way:

```
<return type> <name>(<list of arguments>) {
    <code>
    (if not a void method) return <type>
}
```

For example,

```
int multiplyByTwo(int i) {
    return i * 2;
}
```

Or (||): Or (||) is used in boolean expressions, often in if statements or while loops, and the expression evaluates to true if either one or the other expression (or both) is true. For example,

```
String word = "mississippi";
if (word.contains("a")
    || word.contains("e")
    || word.contains("i")
    || word.contains("o")
    || word.contains("u")) {
    System.out.println(word + " contains a vowel");
} else {
    System.out.println(word + " contains no vowels");
}
```

Primitive types: The objects that exist without the programmer having to do anything. In Java those types are int, char, short, long, boolean, byte, double, float.

Public: An optional word in front of a method definition to signify that it is meant to be used by outside classes. For example, if I have an object Person that has two public methods, getName() and getAge(), I can call getName() and getAge() on any Person object that I create. However, Person may have *private* methods as well. For example, Person may need to do calculations internally to determine what its age is based off of, say, a birthday.

And the `Person` class may want to have a separate method that does that math. But consumers of the `Person` class don't need access to a method called `calculateDays(Date date)` and another method `convertDaysToYears(int days)`. All we care about is that one public method, `getAge()`.

Semicolon (;): A semicolon (;) ends every line of code that is an instruction. For example, a method call, a variable declaration, and a variable reassignment would all end in a semicolon. However, an `if` statement is not an instruction, and so it ends with an open curly brace instead.

Short: A primitive type like an `int`, except it contains half the amount of information. So it can represent numbers between −32,768 and 32,767.

Static: A term used to describe an object or a method on a class that doesn't require an instance of that class in order to run it. For example, if we have an object `Person` and we want to find out the age of that person, we would need to create an object first, and then call `getAge()` on that `Person`. However, we could create a program where we predefine a `static` variable called *EMMY_AGE*, and then we could access Emmy's age without ever creating a `Person` object. We use `static` in our `main` method because our computer needs an entry point into our program. By making `main` static, there doesn't need to be a pre-program that we run in order to create an instance of our `main` object in order to run it.

String: A series of `chars` in order. In code, a `String` is delimited by putting text between quotation marks. For example, `"Hello, World!"`

Variable: A variable is a way of storing a value for use in multiple pieces of a program. A variable can be of any type, and you can reassign it to something else once you have declared it. For example,

```
String name = "Emmy";
System.out.println(name);
name = "Ms. Delaney";
System.out.println(name);
name = "Abigail";
System.out.println(name);
```

If we run this code, we get:

```
Emmy
Ms. Delaney
Abigail
```

Void: A word used to describe the return value of a method that doesn't return anything. For example,

```
void printMultiplyByTwo(int i) {
    System.out.println(i * 2);
}
```

While: Like an if statement, a while loop contains code to execute if a certain condition is true. Before the while loop carries out its inner code, it checks to see if its condition is true. If it is, it will execute its code one time and then check its expression again. It will continue to execute its code while the expression is true. As soon as the condition is false, the computer will move on to the next line of code after the while loop.

For example,

```
void printNumbersOneThroughTen() {
    int i = 0;
    while (i < 10) {
        System.out.println(i);
    }
}
```

Glossary of Music Terms

Adagio: At a slow tempo. In Italian, *adagio* literally means "slowly."

Allegro: At a brisk tempo. In Italian, *allegro* literally means "cheerful."

Andante: At a medium tempo. In Italian, *andante* literally means "walking speed."

Arpeggio: The notes of a chord played in either ascending or descending order.

Augmented fifth: A musical interval that is reasonably pleasing to the ear. It is slightly higher than a perfect fifth, and perhaps slightly less harmonic, but compared to the sound of the diminished fifth, it is the difference between night and day.

Chord: A group of usually three or more notes played together as the basis for harmony.

Crescendo: To get louder as the music progresses.

Diminished fifth: A musical interval that is known for being particularly discordant—so much so that in the eighteenth century it was dubbed *diabolus in musica* or "the devil in music." A diminished fifth can also be referred to as an augmented fourth, or a tritone.

Dissonance: Disagreement, or tension, between two or more notes.

Dolce: Played sweetly. In Italian, *dolce* literally means "sweet."

Etude: A short type of musical composition meant to practice or showcase a specific skill of the player. In French, *étude* literally translates to "study."

Fermata: A symbol, usually placed over some or all of the last few notes in a piece or a section of a piece, to tell the musician that the note is meant to be held longer than its natural length.

Fortissimo: Very loud. In Italian, *fortissimo* literally means "very strong," even stronger than *forte,* which just means "strong."

Four-four time: Also referred to as "common time," four-four time is a description of songs that are written with four beats in a measure. What that means is for every emphasized downbeat, you have three unemphasized upbeats. For example, in a song like "Row, Row, Row Your Boat," which is sung in four-four time, you emphasize every fourth beat of the song.

> *Row*, row, row your boat
> *Gen*tly down the stream
> *Merr*ily, merrily, merrily, merrily
> *Life* is but a dream.

Fugue: A type of song where a repeated phrase is played, repeated, and developed in such a way that it begins to interweave with itself.

Lento: At a slow tempo. In Italian, *lento* literally means "slowly."

Mezzo: In Italian, *mezzo* translates to the word "half." A singer who is a mezzo has a voice halfway between a soprano voice and a contralto voice. Mezzo singers are often women, but do not have to be.

Pianissimo: Very soft. In Italian, *pianissimo* literally means "very quiet." Even quieter than *piano,* which just means "quiet."

Polyrhythm: The simultaneous use of two or more conflicting rhythms that are not a part of the same or related meters.

Presto: A quick tempo. In Italian, *presto* literally means "soon."

Recapitulation: The part of a song or symphony that restates themes from the beginning and middle. Like a reprise.

Requiem: An often mournful song, a requiem is a Mass sung in remembrance, often for the souls of the dead.

Scale: A set of notes, usually spanning a single octave, played in succession, ordered by increasing or decreasing pitch.

Staccato: A note that should be played shorter than its intended length. Marked as a note with a dot above or below it. In Italian, *staccato* literally means "detached."

Subito: As a surprise. In Italian, *subito* literally means "suddenly."

Tritone: Another term for a diminished fifth.

Vivace: At a brisk tempo. In Italian, *vivace* literally means "lively."

Acknowledgments

To quote the acknowledgments section of Carmen Maria Machado's book *Her Body and Other Parties,* "It turns out that when you publish a debut book, you have an impossible task: not just thanking the people who directly influenced this particular title, but thanking everyone who has ever had a hand in your becoming a writer. And, as it turns out, when you sit down and think about it, that list can be dauntingly long." So, first and foremost, to Carmen Maria Machado: Thank you for phrasing my sentiments about this acknowledgments section better than I ever could.

To my agent, Kathleen Rushall: Thank you for helping me realize that Emmy needed to have a musical background herself in order for the story to work. That was my biggest "aha" moment to date and I owe it all to you. Thank you for helping Emmy find her home at Versify, and thank you for being there to answer every one of my emails, whether I was freaking out or asking a bazillion questions. You're a superstar, and I'm so excited to continue this roller coaster together.

To my two editors, Margaret Raymo and Kwame Alexander: Thank you for helping fix all the plot holes I hoped no one would notice. You kept the music front and center, not just in the poetic forms, but in the language itself. Thank you for seeing something in this project, and for seeing something in me. I cannot believe how lucky I am that this book landed at Versify.

To Erika Turner: Thank you for making sure I have a presence on Instagram. I get starstruck whenever I'm scrolling through the Versify feed and I see my picture right beside the other stellar Versify authors.

To Alison Kerr Miller and Celeste Knudsen: Thank you for working with this formatting nightmare! Between my aversion to commas in poetry and the fact that Java has arbitrary rules that are almost-but-not-quite English, it probably made your visual and grammarian sensitivities shiver. But I appreciate you powering through with me and making this book look as much like code, as much like poetry, and as much like English as possible.

To the illustrator of this awesome cover, Abigail Dela Cruz: Thank you so much for bringing Emmy and Abigail to life. It's so cool to literally see the characters I've had only in my head for so long, and I am so grateful for the work you've done making them "real."

To the rest of the team at Versify/HMH: Thank you for everything you do behind the scenes. Thank you for fighting for my book, thank you for making it as good as it could be, and, first and foremost, thank you for making sure that it got into the hands of kids!

To my first semester Hamline advisor, Ron Koertge: Thank you for teaching me to play with poetry. To fiddle with word choice and to ensure that the page is dark with nouns. It's because of you that I know how to craft a simile as sharp as an X-Acto knife.

To my second semester Hamline advisor, Swati Avasthi: Thank you for teaching me that my characters have to come first. Plot doesn't have impact if your characters aren't making choices to move it forward, and my books are better for knowing my characters inside and out.

To my third semester Hamline advisor, Anne Ursu: Thank you for pushing me further than I thought I could possibly be pushed on my critical essay. It taught me that "good" isn't good enough, and that if I really want to be great at something, I have to sit and think and work and rework, and if I put in that legwork, I can achieve things I never thought possible. Thank you for being a voice of encouragement and for truly meaning it when you said "Keep in touch."

To my fourth semester advisor, Laura Ruby: Thank you for letting me scrap my old project and write a novel in verse (which neither of us had ever worked on before) for my creative thesis. You may be surprised that this book is dedicated in part to you, but after working with you on this project for six months, the Ms. Delaney in my head began to look like a combination of you and Ms. Frizzle. In so many ways, this book wouldn't exist without you.

To my Hamlettes, Andrea Knight Jakeman, Barbara Roberts, Blair Thornburgh, Christy Reid, Dori Graham, Jamieson Haverkampf, Jan LaRoche, Lily Tschudi-Campbell, Lily LaMotte, Regina McMenamin Lloyd, and Stephanie Pavluk Wilson: Checking in with this group on Monday mornings got me through every stage of this book. Your encouragement, your faith in me, and your friendship is part of what makes me love writing so much. And every time you get good news, I swear it makes me so happy it's like it's happening directly to me. Thank you for being my Hamline class.

To Blair Thornburgh (again): Thank you for being my writing bestie, for venting with me on Messenger almost literally every day, for planning our weddings together, and for strategizing our lives together. You're on the other side of the country, but sometimes I forget, because whenever something happens during my day you're the first person I message. Also, thank you for reading these acknowledgments and making sure I didn't forget anybody :D :D :D.

To Tasslyn Magnusson: The poetry in this book wouldn't have felt like poetry if it weren't for you. You were my entryway into the world of novels in verse, and if it wasn't for your thoughtful edits and your book recommendations and your multiple reads of this novel, it would be a fraction of the book that it is.

To all my beta readers, alpha readers, and critique partners for this project, Andrea Knight Jakeman, Ariel Pick, Barbara Roberts, Blair Thornburgh, Boggy Fama, Ella Dershowitz, Lisa Riddiough, Miguel Camnitzer Natalie Serrino, Stephanie Pavluk Wilson, Tina Hoggatt, Tim Peacock, and anyone else who read this book in early form: Even if I fought you on your feedback, you were probably right, and it most likely took me six months to notice that. Thank you for making me the best writer I can be.

To the rest of the students, faculty, and staff at Hamline: Whether I was in your workshop or I attended your lectures, whether you help run the program or you participate, whether I follow you on Twitter or we're friends on Facebook, whether you graduated before I showed up or started after I left, whether we've discussed advisor choices or brainstormed a picture book outline, whether we've stayed up until midnight in a dorm room eating pizza and swearing that we'd never get through the next semester, something exists in this book because of you. I love being a part of the Hamline community and I'm so excited to share our writing journey.

To my high school computer science teacher, Baker Franke: Thank you for teaching me Java, and for singing *public static void main string bracket bracket args* to our class. A lot of wonderful things happened in my life because you taught me to code, and even though I'm allowed to call you Baker now, you'll always be Mr. Franke to me.

To my high school English teachers, particularly Carrie Koenen and Sonaar Luthra: Thank you for letting me replace my essay assignments with short stories. Whenever I look back at them, I feel the excitement I once felt when I sat down to write them. And I'm still using the techniques, consciously or unconsciously, that I learned from you . . . and Vladimir Nabokov.

To Elizabeth Fama and Boggy Fama: Thank you for being the reason I started writing. Until our summer 2011 writing challenge, I never thought I could write a whole book. Spending my mornings and evenings (and sometimes even afternoons when I was supposed to be doing my internship) writing taught me how much I love creating worlds in my head. This book wouldn't exist if I had never written that first novel, and I'm so glad I wrote it because it got me here. I'm so glad that we've remained in each other's lives since that first summer. I love going to YA lunch breaks with you, and I love going to your house for dinner, and I love being your friend.

To my college thesis advisor, Joanna Howard: Thank you for taking me on as an honors student. I'm so sorry I made you read that pile of trash so many times. That novel was my first-ever novel and while it belongs in a drawer where it will never again see the light of day, working on it with you taught me that I am allowed to change my words once they're on the page and that when I don't know who a character should be I can't just borrow one from Harry Potter.

To Kwame Alexander (again): Thank you for writing the best mentor book a budding novel in verse writer could hope for. *The Crossover* sat on my desk with me as I wrote Emmy's story, and whenever I wasn't sure how to string words together, or how to turn a page of dialogue into a poem, or how to pace events in my murky middle, *The Crossover* got me unstuck. It means the world to me that I got to work with you on *Emmy*.

To Andrea Davis Pinkney: Thank you for writing *The Red Pencil*, which inspired me to write this book. You may not know it, but your use of colons in that book resembles the way colons are used in the programming language called Python. When I noticed this, I left the gym mid-workout and started writing *Emmy*.

To my sister, Lindsay Lucido: Thank you for letting me know how much Emmy sounds like Aimee. You always keep my ego in check.

To my dad, Gary Lucido: I know you don't really understand why the world of kidlit is important to me, but thank you for reading an early version of this book anyway, and for calling it "interesting."

To my mom, Carol Lucido: Thank you for being my first reader, not just on this project, but on every essay, short story, poem, or novel I've ever written. I counted recently and I think you had read this book, in its entirety, almost fifteen times before it was published. That is, of course, not counting the countless one-off poems I've sent to you to help me line edit, and the dozens of phone calls where I've talked out plot lines to you. This book has my name on it, but honestly, it should have yours, too.

And finally, to my husband, Peter Vulgaris: On our first date I told you how I one day wanted to leave my tech job to become a full-time writer. Thank you for not declaring me insane and for not never wanting to see me again. You made sure I didn't abuse my poetic license on the technical parts of this book, and you kept me honest whenever I was tempted to make my characters too one-dimensional. You're always there with a glass of champagne to toast my wins, and you're always there with a hug and words of comfort to lessen the blow of my losses. Every day I think about how lucky I am to have found you.

Also look for Aimee's newest novel,
Recipe for Disaster.

Recipe for My Family

Mix together
one (1) Mom
   named Liat
   with big curly hair
   she always wears straight
   who works as a biology professor
   at the university across from my school
and one (1) Dad
   named Richard
   with a bald patch
   and a gap between his front teeth
   who works as a financial . . .
   . . . something-or-other.
Bake in Chicago for six years
   at -10 degrees in the winter
   and 110 degrees in the summer
and add one (1) baby boy
   named Samuel
   and love him
   like he's never going to grow up.
Bake for five more years
and add one (1) baby girl

named Hannah
and raise her to be . . .
. . . well, me, I guess.
Bake for five more years
before adding one (1) Grandma Mimi
(my mom's mom)
who will put a whisk in Sam's hand
and a spatula in mine
and it will feel like they've been there
all along.

Bake for seven more years
but be careful
because a happy family
is more delicate than a cheese soufflé:
perfectly balanced
until it's not.

Then, beware
the
f
a
l
l

Fall

Fall

Fall is when we make rugelach.

"In honor of Shira's bat mitzvah!" Grandma Mimi says today.

I lift my spatula in agreement and call out "Hear, hear!" while Sam does the same with his whisk.

My family will take any excuse to bake rugelach. It makes the house smell like fall—butter and chocolate with a hint of cinnamon—and even though no one needs an excuse, it's tradition to come up with one anyway.

Today, that excuse is my best friend's bat mitzvah.

"Hannah?" Dad walks into the kitchen half dressed, waving a folded piece of paper. "Mom wants you to write Shira a note in her card before we all sign . . . ooh, chocolate!" He reaches into the bowl of rugelach filling, card forgotten, and— Slap!

"Ow! Miriam!" Dad licks the chocolate from his fingers. "I wanted to taste your *arugula!*"

Grandma Mimi whisks the bowl of filling off the countertop and points a floury finger toward the door. "On rugelach day, the kitchen is a Jewish space." She says it all stern, but she's laughing as she talks.

Dad waves his sticky hand at me and Sam. "Then what are they doing in here? They're not really Jewish!"

"Rude!" calls Sam, and I laugh.

"My grandchildren?" says Grandma Mimi, tugging at her Star of David necklace. "My Hannah? My Sam? With me as their grandmother, they're as Jewish as they come! Besides, have you seen how they roll rugelach?"

"Yeah, Dad!" I beam at Grandma Mimi and hold up my perfectly crafted rugelach crescent. "We're as Jewish as they come!"

Dad laughs and tries again to reach into the bowl of chocolate filling, but Grandma Mimi pulls it away. "Richard, you're going to make us late. And you, Hannah?" She turns to me. "Go write a note to your friend. Move!"

Dad goes upstairs to get dressed, and I find a handful of colored pencils in the junk drawer.

I write:

<u>Recipe for a She-ra</u>

Mix together:
  my #1 sous-chef
  the nicest person I know
  the Marlin to my Dory
  the REAL winner of the sixth-grade Olympics
        (no matter what Mr. Pierri says)
  Zendaya

(just cuz)
my favorite dance partner
the sister I never knew I needed
and you get one She-ra
(my best friend)

Love,

Ha-na-na-na-boo-boo

P.S. You are the GOAT. And the sheep. And the
cow. Moo.

P.P.S. Remember, if you get nervous, just picture
Jeremy Brewer in his underwear.

Then I draw a picture of us. We're wearing the bat mitzvah
dresses we bought together—caramel for her, green for me—
and we're dancing to our favorite song. It's the one we chose
months ago for the first partner dance of her party: "Single
Ladies."

And with that, I hand the card to Sam to sign.

"When I open my own bakery," he whispers, taking the
card out of my hand, "if anyone pronounces it *arugula* in my
presence, I'm pressing charges."

I laugh. "You better." Then I return to Grandma Mimi's side to finish rolling rugelach, my gift to my best friend on her bat mitzvah.

Rugelach

1C butter

8 oz cream cheese

sugar and salt to taste

1t vanilla

2C flour

butter for brushing

Filling:

For the taste of winter use ~~cranberi~~ cranberries, apples.

In spring use berries: strawberries, blueberries . . .

Summer is ~~peach~~ peaches or plums (stone fruit)

and for fall use chocolate.

Beat butter + vanilla + cream cheese + sugar + salt

Add flour until combined.

Split dough in half and press into circles. Spread filling on
top, cut into triangles. Roll, brush with butter, and bake
at 375 until gold and puffy.

Remember:

Don't be greedy with the filling.

An overfull cookie leaks and burns.

Recipe for a Best Friendship

Mix together
two (2) best friends
  me
  and Shira
  who

        have seen *Finding Nemo*
        forty-one times
  who

        have built more blanket forts
        than they can remember
  who

        have spent five years
        making up recipes
        for Jeremy Brewer Brownies
        Extra Fudge Fudge Ice Cream
        and
        Snow Day Snowballs
  who

        got their braces on at the same time
        even if they won't
        get them off together
  who

have shared every secret
every story
every scheme

who

are never seen one
without the other
except Tuesdays and Thursdays
when Shira has
Hebrew school

who

once left food out for a backyard raccoon
and ended up in the hospital
for emergency rabies shots

who

have baked enough chocolate chip cookies
and Funfetti cupcakes
and strawberry rhubarb pies
with Grandma Mimi
to feed the entire city of Chicago
for one day
or two best friends
for five (5)
years.

Hair

Mom comes downstairs, looking glazed and frosted, frilly and frantic. "You're not dressed, yet? We have to be at Congregation Beth Shalom in an hour! Sam, take a shower! Mom, at least wear an apron if you're going to bake in your new dress! And Hannah, shouldn't you do something with your hair?"

Okay, fine, I get it. Mom's stressing because she hates doing Jewish things.

And okay, fine, I'm sure it also has something to do with the fact that her older sister, Aunt Yael, is a rabbi at Shira's temple, and Mom hasn't seen her in, like, forever.

And okay, fine, it *does* look like Grandma Mimi has rolled around in a sack of flour.

So I get why Mom's anxious.

But did she have to take it out on my hair?

I hate my hair.

It's curly—no, frizzy—no, messy.

Always.

Doesn't matter if I brush it, wet or dry, or if I put hair gel on my comb and swipe it through.

My hair is always . . .

. . . *ugh*.

I wish I could

tame
calm
buff
shine
flatten
straight
my
frizzy
lint ball
dust bunny
cotton candy
hair,
and sometimes I wish for hair
like Shira's.

Dark brown and silky smooth, and she doesn't have to do almost anything before it shines like the mirror glaze on one of Grandma Mimi's cakes.

Maybe I should shave my head, or at least make one of Sam's baseball caps a wardrobe staple.

But today I'll settle for Mom's flat iron.

Family

Shira looks beautiful in her caramel dress. I mean, she's always beautiful, but today she's extra beautiful. Her hair is done in this braid that wraps all around her head, and the way her cousin did her makeup makes her eyes look big and soft. And in her new high heels, she's even standing in a different way than she usually does.

She looks my way, gives me a huge wave, and points to her teeth so I can see her braces are gone.

I give her a giant thumbs-up and smile right back.

"I'm going to say hi," says Grandma Mimi, and at first I assume she's going to say hi to Shira and her family, but Mom says, "Do what you need to do," and I realize Grandma Mimi isn't going to say hi to Shira and her family.

She's going to say hi to Aunt Yael.

Mom mutters something under her breath, and I follow Grandma Mimi with my eyes as she meets a woman I recognize immediately, even though I haven't seen her in seven years: my Aunt Yael.

They talk and laugh and squeeze each other's hands, and when Grandma Mimi gestures over to us, I see Aunt Yael's eyes flicker in our direction.

So I wave.

And why shouldn't I? Grandma Mimi clearly doesn't think she's a terrible person—she takes her out to lunch every month! And it's not like anybody has ever told me why Mom stopped talking to her seven years ago, but I guess Mom thinks I should blindly follow her lead, because as I wave to Aunt Yael, Mom pushes my hand down. "Oh, look at that, Hannah," she says in a voice all high and fake. "I found our seats!"

She grips my hand a little too tight and leads our family to our spot: RESERVED FOR THE MALFA-ADLERS.

Second row, center left.

That's right behind Shira's grandparents but in front of the rest of my class, and three different people—Dahlia Schulte, Jafari Williams, and Jeremy Brewer (who looks extra cute in one of those little round hats they have at the front of the temple)—all ask, "Why do you get to sit up there?"

I smooth out my newly straightened hair and say, "Because I'm basically family."

More from Versify for middle grade readers!